RED LIGHTNING

Red Lightning

LAURA PRITCHETT

A NOVEL

COUNTERPOINT PRESS

Library of Congress Cataloging-in-Publication Data

Pritchett, Laura, 1971-
Red lightning : a novel / Laura Pritchett.
pages ; cm
ISBN 978-1-61902-533-2 (hardcover)
1. Single mothers—Fiction. 2. Families—Colorado—Fiction. 3. Drug traffic—
Colorado—Fiction. 4. Colorado--Emigration and immigration—Fiction.
5. Domestic fiction. I. Title.

Paperback ISBN: 978-1-61902-743-5

PS3616.R58R43 2015
813'.6—dc23

2014048924

Cover design by Debbie Berne
Interior design by Domini Dragoone

Counterpoint Press
2560 Ninth Street, Suite 318
Berkeley, CA 94710
www.counterpointpress.com

Printed in the United States of America

DEDICATED TO

Jake and Eliana

"I felt the grass was the country, as the water is the sea.
The red of the grass made all the great prairie
the color of wine-stains . . . the whole
country seemed, somehow, to be running."

— Willa Cather, *My Ántonia*

"This end won't summarize our forever.
Some things can be fixed by fire,
some not. Dearheart, already we're air."

— Dean Young, "Elemental"

PART I

Wind

Chapter One

What would be the point in confessing a sin for which you had guilt but no real remorse? Bless me, universe, for I have sinned (but I'd do it again in a heartbeat).

*

With Libby I stand a miniscule chance of forgiveness. She looks exactly like I thought she would, too, standing in front of the school with yellow cottonwood leaves dripping down from their treebranch faucets. Exactly ten years older since I saw her last, exactly like a thirty-year-old small-town woman should look, coarse brown hair pulled back in a raggedy ponytail, an oversized white T-shirt and cheapbrand jeans and cheaperbrand white tennis shoes. I watch her from across the parking lot as she chats with a kid who must be my daughter outside the same redbrick squarebox podunk crappy school we went to. A crow squawks, and the blue sky squawks in return. HOME OF THE PIRATES flags flap, and oh, Libby, my sweet sister, you've never seen the ocean, you've never taken something that was unrightfully yours, you've never had to go running across countries. You've put on blinders so as to sweetly sail through the suffering this world offers.

Libby turns in my direction, thinking that, from the corner of her eye, down the street from the school, holykamoly, there's someone who resembles Tess, her good-looking-snarky-trouble-making sister, the sister she hasn't seen for ten years! but no, impossible, this person is too horrible to be her sister, and yet, and yet . . . could it be? Is it a look-alike? Her imagination?

I look past Libby at the kid. Amber. Broad brushstrokes from here. Barrette pulling back a twist of brown hair. Turquoise sweatshirt, red backpack. Senses, perhaps, her mother's intake of breath, turns to stare at me too. In this instant, Libby knows that she could say, "Why, look! See over there? That's your mother, or at least the woman who gave birth to you, whom we haven't seen since, but *she's* not looking like we'd expect, now is she?" But instead she says something along the lines of "Have a good day, dearheart," and gives the kid a nudge, and Amber takes off skipping directly up to a group of ponytailed-backpack-wearing-girls, her twist of hair already breaking loose. Libby turns and stands looking at me across the cracked parking lot and across the cracked years, even after the bell rings and the children's squeals and laughter retreat inside the building and the three yellow swings are left swinging, empty of their energy.

I offer a small wave of the hand. Such a small movement with such potential, and now each of us standing in the new silence, staring at and considering the considerable space that separates us, including a hundred feet and ten years and a thousand different emotions.

Who will take the first step forward?

A gust pelts roadway dirt into my face, but I don't duck and I don't blink. I shift my weight from one foot to the other, push my thumbs into my stomach to stop the ache, hear myself moan a soft surprised sorrow. Still, she doesn't move.

So I do. I take the first step toward her with a *Please don't turn and go* being whispered by every cell of my aching-storming body.

Chapter Two

Bravery is another name for stupidity. If someone knew how difficult something was going to be at the onset, chances are she'd never do it. Brave people are stupid people, and somewhere deep inside, they know and embrace this fact.

Pirates: fighting on a liquid substance that can kill you. Stupid or brave?

Pollos: deciding to cross a dry landscape that can kill you. Stupid or brave?

Love: putting your dusty heart in the care of another. That, too, can kill you.

Motherhood: Libby never would have offered to keep my infant ten years ago had she known the truth back then, which is that the world only pays lip service to the task of parenting. Even kidless me can see that no one has any idea what she is really in for, how she will be broken and smashed.

I walk up to her. My arms reach out on their own; my forehead ducks; I want to plow into her arms, push my head into her chest, a lastditch effort for a redemptive humanhold, but I draw myself up at the last second. Get my spine straight. Her forgiveness is not an assumption I should make. So instead I say, "I didn't stick around because I didn't want to see the results of your stupidity-slash-bravery," and when I see how the sight of me is registering wild on her face, I add, "I've learned one thing in my time, Libby. Well, a few things. But one thing I've learned for sure. I was working this theory out on the bus." I pull a crumpled napkin out of my pocket. The ink has bled into the fibers, and it takes me a moment to make out the words. I have to squint and look off into the sky and cottonwoods and the parking lot before I can return to the napkin. "People protect themselves by withholding their love." I stop here and look at my sister's deepdark shiny doebrown eyes and hold them for a heartbeat. She is still taking me in, gutpunched, and I look back down at my napkin so that the moment can pass unnoticed. "So the thing is, these people think they're being brave and stoic. But of course, they're just cowards. And then what happens is that their love is no longer sought. Everyone forgets they're alive. There's no advantage in rationing it, you see. Rationing emotions and staying quiet kills you. You think you're being brave, but really you're just being stupid." I cram the napkin back in my pocket. "I could die right now, and no one would notice." I stretch my neck one way, then the other, and again, until I hear bones pop. The chain clinks against the flagpole, the pirate flag snaps.

Libby bites a dry fleck of skin from her lip. Now that she's close up, I can see the details. She is still average in her averageness. Height, weight, Kmart-clothes mediocrity. Hair she doesn't dye, strands of white peppered at the very top. Her eyes with no makeup, richbrown as mine and not as striking, but temporarily memorable in the way they look stunned.

"Oh, Tess." She backs up, her eyes watering. "What happened to you? Do you need a doctor? Your cheek." She puts out her hand, nearly touches my grated face, puts her hand back down. "Oh, Tess."

I clear my throat, look off to the sky behind her. "I guess I finally got worn out." My eyes follow a single yellow leaf dance down to the earth. "Like that pirate flag up there, which is pretty tattered. It needs replacing. Why would someone pick pirates to be the mascot of a school in the middle of eastern Colorado?"

"Oh, Tess. Really? It's you? Oh, it is you. Let me take you to the clinic—"

And here Tess hugs herself tighttight.

Tess knows she smells badbad. Blood and vomit and beer and animal body.

Tess wants to howl in a wild voice.

Howl, Tess, howl! Tess should tell her sister that she's gone feralwild.

Is suffocating in her ribcage and in her heartbone.

Tess needs a compass.

North, south, east, west,

AND a moral compass, please.

I crack my neck again. Look at the trees dripping their leaves. Notice the particular hues of yellow, the movement of each individual leaf in the mass of the tree. "I guess I rationed my love. I thought maybe I could give the other path a try. I'm so sorry. I can't stand up anymore." I hear my voice say it, feel my knees buckle, and then I am sitting on the cement sidewalk, fingering the cracks, fiddling with the crumbles. The cool has left the earth all in one moment, and I look around at this new day, now hotter and harder.

She's digging for a cell phone, so I say, "No, no doctor. Please. That's not what I need."

Libby considers this. Considers the money, the fact I might bolt, that I will have no papers, that a doctor and forms will send me into a world I cannot visit. She puts her phone away. "You could just come to work with me. I'm a nurse."

"No. I mean it. That's not what I need."

She takes a deeplong breath in and lets it out in a long quiet sigh. Then she leans over and presses the back of her hand to my forehead, pinches the skin on the back of my hand, feels out my lymph nodes, squats down to peer into my eyes. "You came back to make sure someone would notice your presence on earth? I guess I wish you had another reason. One having a little less to do with you." But she is tilting my head gently one way, then the other. Her eyes run over my body, her finger running across my face. She puts up a finger to see if my eyes track. "You're dehydrated. Your cheek looks like Amber's knees, scraped up like that. It will heal better with ointment to keep it from drying out—"

"—I wish I were that kind of person, Libby. To come back home out of love. But no. I was born without the warm emotions."

She tilts her head sideways at me. "Oh, Tess." Then, "I'm not going to sit down on the sidewalk with you." But she lowers herself next to me on the curb anyway: her jeans and my sweatpants, the bend of knees, and hearts that are bending, too, because here we sat, together, as children, waiting for Kay, here to this very spot we would come, having walked a bit from the school so that we'd be less visible, so that Kay's voice or muffler would not be so loud. Here we would sit, waiting, looking at the school, the weed-filled drygrass park next to it, the post office, the empty lot with cracked asphalt and weeds. Here we are again.

I double over and stare at my crotch and look inside my brain for the spaces and peace that the pot might still be offering. Sitting like this, crisscross-applesauce, even I am sick with the smell of monthly blood and sex in the bathroom of a Greyhound, the smell of beer on the Colorado State hoodie from the dumpster.

I dig my fingernails into my wrist, and Libby leans forward and hugs her knees. She puts her palm over her nose, and into her hand she breathes one of those sighs in which you are collecting yourself, and then, hand still over nose, she looks up to the clearblue sky as if she is searching for patience or compassion there. Her eyes move to one side of the street and then the other, perhaps seeing if there's someone hanging around the shadows, if there is someone watching her sister sit in the middle of the sidewalk.

"I'm alone," I say. "I came alone."

She nods, taking this in. "Well, I didn't expect this. To see you."

"—I know."

"When you left—"

"—I know. It was over, between us."

"No. What I was going to say was, you were so beautiful." She takes her hand from her face and gently touches my face. "It's swollen, too."

Someone revs his truck a few blocks over, there's the distant sound of semi-trucks on the highway, the barking of a single dog, and not a single sound for the blur of tears that rise up in my eyes. We are alone, her eyes and mine. No one is out, the stores haven't opened yet, the kids have been dropped off, and everyone has retreated to allow us this brief flash of time together. My eyes break from hers and focus on one lone figure in the far distance, outside of town, walking a dog and kicking at leaves.

"It's just a missing tooth. I had one pulled the other day." Then, because speaking-attempt is why I am here, I try to continue, although the words bunch up in my throat for a while and my mouth moves in silence, like a newly caught fish gasping for air. Finally, I add, "It hurt so much, and I was so mad at it for hurting, and I didn't have the money for the pain pills, so I got drunk and went up to a stucco wall and scraped my face against it. Just to show it, I guess, that it could hurt worse. Just to show it who was boss. Crazy, right?"

It occurs to me that my sin is that I've never been sorry for being like this. Making a situation worse. Getting pregnant and then leaving the baby for her to care for and then belittling her for doing just that. Getting a tooth pulled and then scraping up my cheek because it was hurting and then hating myself for looking so bad. Lose-lose situation for her, for my face, for everything I have made worse because it hurt.

I look over at Libby in time to see her blink, blink, blink, tears are coming, and she's blinking at the brightblue sky, asking the sky to reverse-rain them away. "I don't know what to do with you. I can see you're still . . . Well, listen. I need to get to work. And by the way, Kay is sick. Very sick."

Kay. White-haired-ponytailed-lousy-mother-Kay. With the green flashing eyes of anger. With the narcissism of a thousand misguided gods. "How sick? Sick enough to die? I bet that is not sitting well with her."

"You should see her. Before." She bites another flake of skin on her lip. "So that's not why you came back? To see Mom? Why did you come back, Tess?"

I look at her left hand, which is, somehow, miraculously resting on my knee, and which has a simple silver wedding band that is catching the light. "You ever think that maybe someone just needs to see home before she can leave again? To clarify the direction she'll take? Well. The only thing I know for sure is that I am tired of sleeping in my car and eating out of dumpsters. I've been camping for a long time, but winter is coming. And I wanted to see my sister. And her baby. Who is not a baby anymore, I can see. My compass just brought me here, Libby. It just directed me here. Homing pigeon. Homing magnet. For just a bit. Don't worry, I won't stay long. At one point, I made a list." Here, I lean to the left so I can dig around in the deep pocket of my sweatpants again, and I pull out a bunch of papers with shit written on them, but I can't find it, so I cram the whole wad of papers back in. "I like lists. They help me think. I learned that from you. I wanted to see Amber. I wanted to see you. I wanted to be honest. I wanted to come here and be as honest as I could and see what happened to you all. So at least I'd know."

A pickup truck pulls up to the curb, and a little kid jumps out. The dad yells, *Ride the bus home, dude,* the kid waves a hand backward at his father, brushing the comment away, and then the father looks at us, pauses, looks again, lifts his hand off the steering wheel in that smalltown wave and drives off.

My hands don't know what to do. I start picking at a cuticle and then scratching my wrist, and then I sit on my hands, trying to cage the birds that they are. "So, sorry. I'm nervous. I saw Amber. What grade's she in?"

"Fifth. You smell . . . Tess, you smell . . . like you're rotting. I'm sorry. But it's true. Let's get you somewhere . . ."

"Ms. Skeek still teaching?"

"Nope."

"Amber a smart kid? Healthy?"

"Yep."

"Like you."

"Smarter and healthier than either of us ever were. That's the truth." She regards her hands, now both in her lap, fingers laced. While she's looking down, I look at her sideways to see a crooked wet stream across her face. The water zigzags down, just like the cotton-wood leaves zigzag down through sky above her. She doesn't try to stop, and she doesn't apologize. Instead, she waits, and I wait, and the tree waits, and we all wait under the pulsing blue sky.

She breathes in very slowly, finally recalibrating. "Amber knows about you. That you gave birth at the hospital and took off the next day."

"Good." I don't argue the point. I did come back once, to sign the papers and make it all official. I did hold that infant kid then.

"That you haven't stayed in touch. Not even a birthday card." She glances at the school, back at me. "I've always just been clear with her. No use in lying. Wouldn't know what to say anyway. This is her first week. School just started. She's got enough to worry about already." She wipes her face with her forearm. "You homeless? Where are you staying?"

The yellow swings on the playground have ceased to move. They just hang there, useless, and I say, "It doesn't matter. I don't care. A tent. A car. I'm sorry I didn't call. I'm not really in a place where I can . . . I dunno, uh, think ahead. I don't have a phone, I don't have money to make a call, I have absolutely nothing, Libby. Nothing." I squint at her, and then my eyes go back to the swings. "No-thing, noth-ing, n-othing, not-a-thing." I singsong it to myself, a little hum, a little prayer, a little accusation to the universe. "Not-a-thing-at-all."

Libby clenches her jaw, meaning she's hardening up and done with the tears. "I can't just—Tess. How high are you? How sick are you?" When she gets no answer, she adds, "I don't know if I want Amber to see you. Or you her. Or if I do, I'd like to prepare her, you know?" She stands and reaches her hand out to pull me up. "Although I don't know how to do that, prepare her to see you."

I ignore her hand and stand up on my own, my knees aching with the effort of it. I scratch my arm, look at a yellow sweatshirt that has been abandoned by the chain-link fence. Wonder if it would fit me. Listen to some teacher inside clapping and guiding kids with *the wheels on the bus go round and round*, and their little voices chiming in. "I'll give them this much," I say, nodding in their direction. "Their voices actu-ally sound like blooms, yellow flowers, dancing in the air."

She shakes her head no, sweeping my comment away. "How did you get here, anyway? You walked here from the highway? The gas station? Isn't that the Greyhound bus stop?"

"Indeed it is, and yes. I had the distinct pleasure of walking down the highway and through Mainstreet-NoWhere-Colorado with exactly one grocery, one post office, one closed-up movie theatre, one church, one shitty city park, and one brick library, all the exact fucking same. This place is so poor, so dried up. I knew I'd eventually find you here. Boneknowledge."

Libby runs her hand over her eyes, rubs her forehead. "Oh, Tess. That's too long of a walk. You must have been walking for hours. You don't have a backpack? Luggage?"

"Got not a single thing." I don't tell her about my feet, which are bleeding inside my shoes, don't tell her about the inside of my throat, which is a desert, don't tell her about the inside of my stomach, a roiling burnache, and not my chest, which is a universe of spiraling stars.

"You sound crazy." She tilts her head at me, considering this fact, and when I don't answer, she says, "Okay. I'm going to at least get you some food and water and a shower. I'm going to take you home. Just so you know, I'm married." She clears her throat to get my attention, and so I look up. "I got married to Ed."

"He still a hippie beekeeper? Still drive that orange VW bus around?"

"Yup."

"Those cute little John Lennon glasses. I always figured he smoked a lot of pot."

"As it turns out, no."

"He's older than you."

"We stayed friends for a few years until it became obvious. And by then, age didn't matter. He's been an excellent father to Amber. He's a good human being."

"Deepgood? Heartsweeper?"

"Yeah." She smiles a little at that. "I can see you're still inventing words."

"You got other kids?"

She hesitates. "Nope. Amber has been enough." She starts walking to her pickup, waves to me with her arm. "Well, come on, then. Crazy or not, I need to get you somewhere."

I follow her. "Libby? We know how to reboot a computer. But is there a way to reboot a person? To start again?"

She shakes her head. "Cut it out, Tess. That's enough. I can't ever figure out if you're being earnest or a jackass. And neither can you. You have the capacity for the first, but you always fall into the second. I can't deal with that right now. I have to get to work. I can't take the day off, not this late. People depend on me. Even if I haven't seen my own sister for ten years. We have to figure something out." But then she stops, turns to look at me, still unbelieving. "Please don't talk to me on the way. Just sit there, quiet. Just let me drive and get over the surprise of this. I just can't believe it. I just can't—"

"I can be quiet. Quiet like you would not believe." I sound confident, but when I breathe out, there's the vibration of all the fear I've been housing. My ribcage moans in response, sore with the effort of this big of an exhale, of the travel and coughing, of the effort of having to house my messy heart. I want to buckle over with the heavypain of it. But at the exact same time, I know the vibration is also from lightrelief, because what if going home was a gal's lastditch effort? And if it didn't work, if she got shunned, she'd have to play the hand she's been carrying around in her back pocket as a last-resort option? And she can see that now she's at least got a bit of time before she uses that final tool in her extremely limited toolbox? I want to buckle under the relief of that, too.

I don't buckle. Instead I follow her like an obedient dog and climb in an old black Ford truck that has schoolbooks and a jump rope on the floor, a stack of mail on the dash, a cow's yellow eartag. Thank god. Thank some god for my sister, who seems to be willing to keep her heart open for at least a moment despite all the very good reasons not to, proving, I suppose, that we humans are kinder and more generous than whatever god struck us into life.

Chapter Three

The grasses in the fields run in waves alongside the truck, breathing and moving together, a symphony, a cadence, a yellowdance. Like an ocean, and here we are, its pirates. That same wind makes my hair shift across my face, soft on my swollen jaw. We pass a group of heat-worn horses, standing exhausted. We pass round hay bales, an abandoned pickup truck, hot pastures that stretch on into the horizon. There's a bailer in another field, boxing up pastureland, and antelope in the far distance stand paused and surprised by life. It all looks exactly the same. Exactly like it did ten years ago when I first drove away, next to fields exactly like this, with my hair whipping around my face. I wonder what it is I've come back to be forgiven for. Perhaps knowing what I was about to do—and doing it anyway.

I sat in the passenger seat while a man drove me off, and I knew exactly what I was doing:

—I was climbing in a truck and leaving my squawking red-faced
  infant

—with my sister, an unattractive loser version of myself living in a
shithole house in the middle of NoWhere, Colorado,

—with our mother, mean and abusive (from being abused herself,
but still),

—and I was confining them to the very life that I was hightailing
it out of there to escape,

—and I didn't feel any emotion whatsoever for any of them,

—the place where emotions reside being long ago wiped nearly clean,

—though one sliver of emotion remained, a sliver as thin as the
smallest fingernail moon, and it was telling me that the best way
to love was to leave.

I look over at Libby, who is crying silently as she drives, and then
look back the other way to the earth. Fields, sky, a line of cottonwoods,
the outline of mountains in the distance, blurred by haze. We turn a
corner, and a few of the cows gathered around a stock tank raise their
heads to me in a gesture of cow-interest. I stare back. Perhaps one sort
of love does not block another; love is a capacity that grows by use, and
I'll start with the cows. I've always admired them, their stupid calmness, how that calmness is so solid that one is convinced of the absence
of an inner life. Plus the way they lick out their noses with their tongues.

I sigh and look back at my sister. Bless me for being like you, god.
Bless me for being either insane or unjust or cruel. Bless me for creating
suffering and then turning away from it, for pretending that I wasn't
leaving a swath of pain raging like a fire in my wake.

*

"Those are Amber's 4-H heifers." Libby blinkers, and we slow. The cattle are standing in the V of the corner between the county road and a long dirt driveway, flicking their tails against the flies, chewing their cud. A cluster of cottonwood trees blocks what must be her home up ahead. "Usually we sell them, but this year we won't. We'll breed and milk them. We make cheese." She slows again for the potholes and washboard of a driveway, and my ribs ache. I push the last of the offered granola bar into my mouth, chewing on one side, the bloody tissues mixing in, then slosh my mouth with warm water from an aluminum water bottle. My body jolts with the bumps, too weak to brace against the onslaught of the earth, and all I can think is, *This should feel familiar, Tess, because all those you have transported around have felt this way.*

Libby pulls into the center of the gravel circle that is surrounded by various buildings. She puts the truck into park, pushes the truck door open, swings herself out, is soon outside my side, waiting. I sit. Bedazzled. Unable to move. In front of me is a curved home, an oval of sorts, glistening blue and green bottles. I blink, squeeze my eyes shut, try again. Here is *The Lord of the Rings*. No, *The Hobbit*. What kinda pot did that guy give me on the bus? I close my eyes, open one and then the other, trying to see it all again.

Libby opens the truck's door for me. "It's called an Earthship."

"This is where you *live?*" I hear myself murmur, "Well, I'll be. Holyshit." I sit, taking in the arches and swoops, although it's the textures of this home that keep stopping my eyes up. Rough adobe. Glass. Smooth. Glinting. My eyes are complaining: they're too scratchy, too tired, and yet they're looping all over the place, following the swoops and glints and colors. "I've seen these down by Taos. I just never expected one here. There are tires in there, right? I mean, your house is made out of tires? And bottles? And aluminum cans? Looks like something a wizard would live in."

"Or us." Libby stands at the truck's door, holding out her hand so as to help me out.

"And it works on its own, right? Like, it doesn't need the rest of humanity—"

"It has its own water catchment, generates its own electricity, yes. Off the grid."

My eyes follow the facts, which is how one thing leads to another: the curves of the Earthship lead to prayer-flags, and those lead to an adobe chickenhouse with more prayer-flags, which take me over to a stack of beehives. Then a small corral, then donkeys, which start braying as soon as I turn to look at them, and they're loud enough to crack my head in two. I circle round, looking at the whole sweet-strange homestead.

"I turned out to be a hippie." Libby laughs, and my head jerks toward her in surprise. Her laugh means something. It means she has let go of the anger and the nervousness and the stress for just a moment, and it is thus an act of generosity, and it feels like another punch, her laugh being one that reminds me of all the young versions of us, play-ing at a home near here but the very opposite of this—unbeautiful inside and out—the memory flooding into me now of her laugh back then, our laughs being generated from barn cats or the burn barrel or by running through the purple-blooming alfalfa fields with kites. Back when we had laughs worth letting out of our bodies, back when laugh-ter was possible in the unbeautiful. "Laughter is carbonated prayer," I say. "I heard that once. This house is like carbonated building materi-als. This place is like a crazyass womb."

Libby gives me a look of tender confusion. "You and your . . . observations. I like it here, too." She looks around the place herself and then out at the dry grassland fields that run in every direction.

"And there's Ed—which is good, because, really, I have to get to work. I want to see you, Tess. But there are people who need me. Literally and immediately."

A question comes flying out of me that surprises the both of us. "But do you love him, Libby? Do you have that emotion?" But what I'm wanting to ask, or, rather, confirm, is that it's not true, is it? Love? That in truth they die a little to each other each day, right? She loses more of herself to the mundane stupidity of cow-life, yes? That secretly, her life is empty and boring and cardboard-like, yes? Even in a magical place like this?

I glance from the dancing prayer-flags to her eyes, and it's the way the skin around them crinkles that tells me the most. That's where the changes of the last ten years have found themselves. What they show me is that she has an ownership of herself. "Yes, I do love him, Tess." She says this as we watch Ed, who is registering surprise as he recognizes me and as he walks up to us: pause, go, pause, head-duck, go. He's in jeans and a stained white T-shirt, sandcolored curly hair and little glasses, taking off work gloves, wiping his forehead with his forearm. "I love him," she says again, quickly, before he arrives. "I love it when he holds me in his arms and reads to me at night. I love the way his front teeth overlap just the tiniest bit, I love the curve of his smile. I love when he gets indignant. I love when he leans over Amber's homework to help her. I love when he's tired and he gets his feet under him anyway. He's the most mindful person I've ever met. Do we annoy each other? Yes. Is it sometimes hard? Yes. But Tess, he is the opposite of what we knew, he is a gift of grace." She looks at her watch and says, "Don't tell him any of that, though. Right now we're in a fight about when to extract the honey. And I gotta get to work. That's the reality. So I'd just like to know, are you planning on leaving? As in, if I go to work, will I see you again?"

I falter. "Yes. You'll see me when you're off work. If you allow it."

All this gets voiced in a fast moment, and then Ed is there in front of me. We take each other in. He looks stricken, but all I can think as I drift my gaze across him is some people don't age, and Ed is clearly one of them. He looks exactly like he did ten years ago, that light curly hair and calmsleepy eyes, and yes, the left side of his smile has the slightest tip curve upward, but his smile is one of confusion, not joy, and it disappears when he turns in my direction. Behind him appears a dark mutt that darts up to me and lets out one single bark.

"Quiet, Ringo." Libby reaches down and scratches the dog's ear.

"But Ringo was the name of the dog you had before."

"All dogs around here are named Ringo."

"That's not very inventive."

"Tess?" Ed's eyes dart from me to Libby and back at me. Then, bless him, he walks closer, holds out his hand, then backs up at the smell, puts his hand in his jean pocket, tries to recover, puts his hand back out for me to shake. Which I do. "Tess. It *is* you. I guess I . . . didn't . . . recognize—" There's a long pause, and then he says, "Well, last time I saw you, you were running those *ilegales*. You were in a bit of trouble, as I remember it." Sincerequiet voice. I glance at Libby. That's why she loves him. He's a *man*. Gentle but can stand under pressure and hold his ground.

I look right back at him. He has changed too. Not in looks but in solidness. He's not mousy like I remember. "No one says *ilegales*, Ed. It's *smugglingwetbacks*. All one word. You should know that." It comes out bitchier than intended, so I try for something more tender. "The last time I saw you, you were holding baby Amber. I see she's grown up now." And then, because his eyebrows shoot up, I add, "I saw her from a distance. Just a distance."

He takes off his glasses with one hand, rubs his eyebrows together with the other. "Well, you're not looking so good, frankly. Which makes me want to ask, what's changed for you?"

It's the hesitation that gives me away—the surprise of that question being asked so soon. I can't even get my brain to focus on one of the answers I had ready.

> Tess only needs to recover from all those empty universe
>> spaces,
> from the pot,
> from lack of sleep,
> from wheels on the bus going round and round.
> The question of death.
> The inevitability of human oblivion.
> How can most everyone ignore that
> fact except Tess?
> To walk so close to death but
> move through life as if that's not true?
> Tess doesn't get it.
> Why it doesn't crack everyone in two.

I glance at the sky, back at him. "Wait, what? What did you just ask me? Am I still smuggling wetbacks? Is that what you want to know?"

But his face has already turned hard. "Libby, I don't want her here. She doesn't deserve it."

I throw my arms out, wide, like I am embracing the air, to stall for time. "Or are you really asking me something else? Are you really wondering if life on the margins has a sharper pain, if I've suffered enough yet?"

He leans forward, and his voice is low. "What I want to know, Tess, is what danger are you bringing to our home? And I want to know it now."

"I'm trying to be honest of late. You want to know what I've been up to? Here's a quick summary." I am talking fast, before he can get another word in. I had this practiced on the bus. The words are stuck in my throat and garble around for a moment but then start to leak out. "Yes, I was a part-time *levantona*. It was lucrative, me being a female driver and all. But I stayed on the outskirts, Ed. That was true, even back then. I was always on the periphery. Never that much in the know. Which gang was which gang, so on, so forth. I purposefully stayed away from all that. I just did the driving within Colorado. Or nearby. I had a gun, I could use it, I'm tough enough. But I only did small and safe groups. Kind of like . . . well, kind of like staying with pot and not going to meth. I stuck with the safe transports, ones that had been weeded through by my friend Slade. Whatever route I was told. So my knowledge of the whole shebang is surprisingly limited. But I recently decided to do just one more trip . . . for the money . . . because somehow it always goes. I needed cash to start fresh. Because I was hungry. Not as in, man, I need a snack. But as in, I'm going to die if I don't get some food—"

Ed makes a circular motion with his hand, a speed-it-up. "I want the truth before I ask you to leave. What kind of situation are you in?"

Libby starts to say something, but I interrupt her and keep my eyes on Ed. He's the one who will need convincing. "A group was coming in this past week. In the mountains near Alamosa. With *coca y mota*—because now they're more or less required to carry stuff. So this guy, Lobo, he's the *coyote*, a *culero*, the head honcho, you know, *el pollero*, it's his men who get everyone across the U.S.–Mexico border. *My* job is just to pick them up in the mountains and get them to Denver. That's all. No big deal. I especially move women and children. I just drive and stay out of it. ICE is just a bunch of fuckers these days, and you know, being a *gringa*—"

"What I want to know, Tess—"

"—The freakin' *pollos* didn't show, Ed. I don't have anyone with me." I look toward the mountains so he can't see my eyes. I don't know how much longer I can stand up. How much longer my heart can possibly beat. The granola bar has awakened a giant, and the giant is roaring for food and is thrashing, thrashing, thrashing, and if only I can stay calm a little longer. "They didn't show. I was at the right place. I waited for three days. They didn't show. So I came here. The end."

A flash in the air—Ed and Libby share a glance of something deep like a river, an energy, something big enough to send out a flash of feeling, and it startles me.

"Wait, what . . . you—" Ed starts, but Libby interrupts him with a palm that flies up, a shake of the head, *no*. "We can't talk about this now. Let her take a shower."

I glance back and forth, trying to figure the energy out. "I came here," I finally say into the silence, "for three days. Then I'm out of here. Heading east this time, actually. Gonna disappear into the flat-lands of the middle of this country. But stay three days with you guys, that's what I wanted. If you'll have me. If not, I'll take off now. No one is with me."

"Tess, Tess, Tess." Ed has recovered and puts his hands in his hair and rubs his scalp. "We can't have that sort of thing around here. We have a *child*, we have *Amber*—" He throws his hands in the air. "You never understand the gravity of anything! We can't have someone who is involved in trafficking here. *Comprende?*"

"Well, so, that's what I'm saying. I'm done with it. I just came for a short visit. And then I'll leave." I hear the shake in my voice, feel the tremor up my spine. I hear also what I am not saying, which is: I did that run for Amber. To leave her a bit of money. To leave a small evidence of my existence. But I couldn't find the damned people, and I never got paid, and now I have to disappear for good without leaving her anything at all.

Libby and Ed stare at me, and I stare at my feet, shift my weight. Finally, Libby says, "I have no idea what to do with this . . . and I gotta change Kay's bag . . . and I gotta get to work. I just can't—"

Ed's hands are still at his temples, rubbing. "I'll do Kay's medicine. You go."

The world is so heavy, my body so heavy, my eyelids so heavy. My feet hurt, my mouth hurts, my bones hurt, and the world is spinning, and my mind is retreating away from my body, moving into the sky. I feel my body sink down, lean over, sideways, feel the gravel under my cheek. I close my eyes.

> In the Beginning and Once Upon a Time,
> there was baby girl born in the
> Kingdom of Colorado,
> a sweet child named Tess.
>
> Who grew up and each year got more messed up,
> perhaps because of slaps and screams
> or alcohol
> or the boyfriend or two (boyfriends of the mother, that is)
>   finding ways to open her up
>
> or because she was not strong enough to keep her chin up
>   in this life.
>
> This Tess became a pirate. A land pirate.
>
> Then she sailed to a place and she saw something that
>   killed her.
>
> And that's when
> Tess one day found herself looking down at herself instead
>   of inside herself.
>
> At the End, of this particular story,
> Tess had to go.
> She had gotten surrounded.

Had to surrender.

But this girl, Tess, had already begat another girl named
Amber.

And Tess wanted to tell her goodbye.

I dig my fingers into my arm in order to try to come back, but I keep my eyes closed. At first there is silence, and then murmurs that do not involve me. *Go on in to work, Libby. They need you. I'll deal with this. I'll figure something out . . .*

Get her some food, at least . . . a shower.

I'll call you. Let me see what's going on here.

Let her sleep . . .

I'll call you . . . A doctor?

We'll talk later today. Let's just leave her here at the house for now. There's nothing she can really do.

We can't leave her alone with Amber. Can you be here when she gets off the bus?

I open my eyes to see Ed holding Libby's head to his chest, his head bent so he can whisper in her ear, hers raised to whisper back, and if ever there was a position of love, that is it.

I slap the gravel, hard, with my palm, to stop my inside voices: I want the vocalchord voice. I do not want them to see how bad off I am. "I'm not going to hurt or kidnap Amber," I hear myself say. "If you could just let me rest."

"Go," Ed says firmly to Libby. "I'll work it out. I'll call you."

I hear the truck door slam, the pebbles of the driveway crack and snap, the murmur of retreating tires. When she's driven off, Ed gets on his hands and knees so that his head is right across from mine. I think that maybe he'll reach out and touch my head and bless me, but he does not. He waits until I open my eyes and look at him. Stare, stare, blink. A good coupla minutes go by. Finally, he props a water bottle next to my face. "Drink this. Do you or do you not need a doctor? Answer me now."

"I do not," I say to the pebbles in front of my mouth. "I need sleep and food."

He nods, agreeing with me. "I am trying. To. Find. Lovingkindness." Then, "Oh, Tess, you can't—" Then, "Say something, anything, to help me find some warmth. I'm human, too, Tess. With my own limitations. I can see you're suffering. But you've also caused so much of it . . ."

I don't move my head from the gravel, even when my ear and jaw hurt from the talking. "Ed. I've got a side to the story. And it is influenced, in part, by you. The good comes from you. I'm helping the immigrants start a new life. Right? Like you once did. You taught me." The scrape on my cheek is opening up from the movement of my jaw, but still I don't move. "So, Ed, for example, I always dropped off water and tennis shoes whenever I was in the middle of nowhere. Because, you know, you and Libby . . . last time I saw you, ten years ago, you said to . . . you know, act like a human because I was dealing with humans. They're not just *pollos*, chickens who need to be crossed by the *coyotes*, they are individual lives, with loves and dreams and stories. You told me that once. I remembered."

He puts his hand gently on my skull, on my greasy matted hair. "Yes, Tess. And there are kind people, and there are *dangerous* people. You know that better than I. You're dealing with people who kill. And you come here, to your own kid's home? I'm worried because you've often been so naive. I need to know the status. Anyone pissed at you? Is anyone coming after you?" He pulls his hand away. "Sit up, Tess. Get up off the driveway."

Brainspeed, please. Find a multisplendored lie. The chunks of gravel in front of me are beautiful: blues and grays and whites. "I'm done. I brought no trouble. I'm really done." I can hear the dream in my voice, from the crazy place, from the fluid nature of being nearly gone. "But you know, Ed? I did something smart," I singsong. "I remember lying to Lobo, he's the *coyoteprimero*. I told him I was from Oklahoma, from a town called Normal, and that's why I was so messed up—get it, that sad joke? And that was ten years ago, when I was first getting started. Slade might guess where I am, but that's okay because he's a good man, a little like you, actually, sometimes doing things for the right reason. I've been homeless since . . . I don't know . . . last spring. No one knows where I am. That was really going to be my last job, Ed. I wanted to be done with that life. I just needed one last bit of money for a new start."

"This Lobo. He really doesn't know where you are? There's no way he can track you?"

"I'm not *stupid*, Ed." And now I can hear my voice rising to a higher pitch. "Who knows what happened to that group of people? I'm sure someone picked them up. I don't know. Probably they got to Denver. And the drugs got to Lobo. No one knows where I am. No one is after me. So just tell me. Can I stay for a few days or not?"

Ed's face flashes a reluctant storm. "I just . . . don't understand how you can be so unkind, Tess." His voice is calm but somehow still full of rage. "You abandon your sister and your baby and your mother, and you don't keep in touch *at all*? Except postcards once every two years proclaiming you're alive? Do you understand the things you set in motion? By your neglect? The things you didn't do? Never a birthday card to Amber. Never a Christmas card. You know how that made her *feel*, what trouble it has caused?" He stands up with a grunt, brushes off his knees, throws his arms out and walks in a tight circle, and then comes back, facing me. "It's just that I think your core is *rotten* in ways I don't understand. I know you had it bad, Tess. But that's not an excuse for leaving Amber, for ditching immigrants in the mountains, whatever you've done that landed you here." He stops, looks to the sky as if begging it for patience, exactly like Libby did earlier, and it occurs to me that she learned this from him. He glances at the Buddhist flags and does some deep breathing. "Man, you are the only person on Beautiful Planet Earth who could get a rise out of me. I don't usually—" and here he stops and puts his head in his hands again and breathes. "I don't want to be the one who threw away the chance for you to meet Amber. I don't want that hanging on me. I suppose you should." He breathes in. "Look, I need to bring in the bee boxes, I need to check on some neighbor's animals, I need to fix some fence, but I'll make sure I'm home in the afternoon. Libby is one of the few nurses still over in town these days—that town is dying—and if she doesn't go in, then the people get no help. Do you see? Do you see that she has to go because she's got a responsibility? Because there's no one else to do it? Like raising a child?"

"I came to say thanks—"

"I'm going to leave you alone till this afternoon. Sleep and eat and drink and shower. Amber will get off the bus at three forty. I'll talk to her, and if she's willing, I'll let you guys hang together." He nods, agreeing with himself. "I'm thinking aloud here as I go. Are you listening? You will be kind and considerate of her feelings before you consider your own. You will sit down or take a walk and ask her about her life. You will not talk of *pollos* and *coyotes*. If she wants you to leave, I'll take you to the bus station over in Lamar. If she wants you to stay, we will all have dinner together. You will explain to her why you never sent a birthday card or a Christmas card or anything. You got it?" He pulls out a wallet, crams some bills under my arm, where they're pinned down from the breeze. "If you want to leave earlier, here's some money for the bus."

"I got it." And then, "Ed? That's what . . . I came here for. No one has asked *why* I came—"

He throws up his hand like he doesn't want to hear. He walks away from me, opens the door of an old green Harvester truck. "You came because you didn't have anywhere else to go." He turns his head over his shoulder to say this to me. "There's nothing much here to steal, so don't even bother looking. There are twenty more bucks in my sock drawer; take it if you want it. Make yourself at home, though. Eat. Take a shower. Put on some of Libby's clean clothes. We have to truck in water, though, so take it easy. Strip at the door in case you've got lice or bedbugs, then take your clothes to the burn barrel. You look . . . lousy."

I roll over to my back. "The clouds are pretty from here."

He climbs in his truck, backs out, walks back, reaches down, touches my forehead. "I'm just noticing—how much pain are you in?"

I move my face so I can look at his eyes. "I feel great. I don't need a doctor. I just need sleep."

His hair lifts a fraction in the breeze. He reaches out his arm. "Ringo is in the truck. I'll take him with me. Let me help you up. Go on inside."

"No, I want to get up on my own."

He sighs. "See, you think you're being tough right there. But really, you're being selfish. That, Tess, is what is so hard to forgive about you. You don't want to give me the peace of mind that you're safe inside. I can't very well just leave you lying here in the hot sun in a gravel driveway. Help me out, here." He regards me. So for his benefit, I push myself to my hand and knees, and then, slowly, stand. The world tilts a little, my feet start pulsing with their ache. He puts the water bottle in my hand, nods approvingly.

I watch him pulling out of the driveway, the tires snapping gravel, and I want to shout something after him. Something along the lines of: Guess what, I'm in so much pain that I can't believe my body is still here. Guess what? I've come here to at least pretend to be human, I can do that, and I can at least put up a show. Guess what?

I've come here to have one more burst of flame, of wildfire, of life, one more rage-against-the-night, and tenderness is the last whisper of a breeze on the embers.

When he's out of sight, I sink down till my knees touch gravel, and I bash my forehead into the rocks. I never thought a person could end up so alone.

Chapter Four

Sleep. I wake in a not-enough-air panic, naked body sweat-covered. My throat is too tight, and so I gasp, stumble up. Stand, hunched over and breathing, and then sink back down to the floor, my knees giving way to the gravity that sucks at them. I sleep again. Wake again. Regard my naked body again. That bruise, and that one? That purple one, that yellow one. Where did I get them? Where am I? Where are my clothes? Oh, they're outside, and I'm inside a strange Earthship, colors glinting in on me, on the bright colors of a mostly red rug. I reach up to touch the pulse on my forehead, feel out the bump. I feel my hairline dripping water and grease, I feel the slide of a bit of blood where my forehead hit gravel. My tongue feels out the gaping hole in my mouth and presses against the nerve-jangly ache. I sink back down and regard the colors around me.

Sleep.

Wake.

When I open my eyes to the bright red softness I am on, sunlight is pouring in from the window. *Sunlight out of water*, my brain sings, and my eyes are not so sore, the sequencing of thoughts has been turned on, my self is in my body. I sit up, slowly, and regard my feet. I must have left my tennis shoes outside, too, but I don't remember taking them off, how I managed to unstick them from my bloody heels. I stare at my feet now, swollen, streaked with dried blood, the circles of skin that mark the edges of blister. I ask them: *Will you carry me? Please?*

They comply and hold my weight, walk me down a hallway. My fingers trace the wall for balance. I find a bathroom, step inside the shower, stand in the heat until the sting of cuts and scrapes blooms and then fades. I find shampoo and try to untangle my hair, then soap my body and soap again.

I stand naked in front of a large mirror. I am too tired to be surprised, although not too tired to make note of that fact. My jutted ribs, the lack of fat on my ass, the scrapes on my side, the rise of hipbones, the raised welts of some rash, the bruise that runs down one thigh. I peer closer. My scraped check, the swell beneath it, the bump and blooming bit of blood on my forehead. My eyes, seeking myself. My pupils, tiny black holes adjusting themselves ever so slightly, the brown iris around, the blink of long eyelashes. *Hey, 'less, do you see anything? Anything beautiful left in there?*

I wince and step back quickly. In a drawer I find scissors, and I cut my tangled hair into a bob and work with it until the brush runs through. The slices of hair fall in wet, scraggly tangles with one clean-cut edge. I find a pair of Libby's clean underwear and sweatpants and a tank top and a T-shirt, and I pull them on.

Back in the bathroom, I sit on the toilet seat and rub lotion into my desert skin. I rub ointment into my feet, rub a swath on my crotch in the hope it might help the ache that is thrumming there. I find a pad of Libby's and stick it in my underwear to catch the blood that keeps seeping. I stand to gingerly brush my teeth, lift my lip so that I can see the raw tissue, see there is a pocket of pus, and swish my mouth out with peroxide and water. I look at myself again. Think: *Morality is something we can smell on people, and you still stink.*

*

All life starts in the kitchen, but I cannot find any alcohol in any of the cupboards to start my endeavor. I turn on the radio in search of distraction or news, but it's not the right time of day, and there's only country-western. I crack my neck to try to work out The Antsy and The Nervous. I offer myself a banana and a cracker and some kind of fizzy iced tea that I find in a jar in the fridge. I offer it all carefully to my body. I offer myself ibuprofen from a bottle I find in the bathroom, Percocets I find tucked in the back of their nightstand, underneath some pillowcases and reading glasses.

Now I barefoot-wander the house, into the strange nooks and crannies, the sunroom, the tomatoes and basil growing out of hydroponic plastic bottles. My feet pad over the hard smooth gray floor, wander into rooms of jeweled sunlight made by different-colored wine bottles. There is a pattern to the colors of this house, and it takes me a moment to place it. North-facing walls are all a purple blue, the west walls are sage, east are peach, south are yellow. I remember this, something about the best way to capture sunlight, make every angle pleasing to the eyes.

I end up in front of the mirror again to doublecheck Tess is there. The room is well lit with a bright burning series of bulbs, and it is clean and only has a small clutter of knickknacks-of-selfcare, and beyond that is a woman in a mirror.

> The eyes of Tess are so darkbrown liquid shiny and still
>> they are there.
> Tess remembers her eighteen-year-old self,
> fine dark hair whipping around her face

as she leans out the truck's window and sing-songs *goodbye,*
    Libby, goodbye, take care of that baby, I'm driving off with mine,
smiling at herself in the rearview mirror,
smile with a dimple, beautiful teeth, dark alive eyes, gor-
    geous hope,
as if that man and that truck were going to take her great
    places,
as if she herself were special
and was called into this world for great glory.

Gut-punched with a memory? I didn't think it could punch so hard. But it can. I hold my stomach, cradling the hipbones with my palms, as if inside were a baby. *Hold steady, kid. Three days to make it right.*

*

The wheat flour is in a large glass container. Eggs, butter, baking soda, cinnamon, but no such thing as sugar. Only honey. I drink water and eat crackers and murmur to myself:
    Of course there is no sugar in this house,
    of course I will have to guess how much honey,
    of course that will ruin whatever it is I'm making,
    of course there's no alcohol,
    of course.

I stir the liquid gold into the batter and think: *The people who make it in the world are those who can* of course *it.*

Of course life is harder than you thought. Of course babies die, unbirthed in their mother's pelvic bones. Of course pirates come, of course people get lost at sea. Of course Libby's house is clean and clutter free, Libby who was always tempering the mess as a kid, the catshit and black widows and flies and toilet smell and overflowing trash and cigarettes and Kay's empty beer bottles everywhere and even Kay's vomit. Of course I let Libby do all that because even though I noticed it all too, and I hated it, I let Libby be the one who kept trying to bring back order and beauty.

I stir until my arm aches. How come people never speak of this? How much the body can hurt? The mindwhir? How much work it takes to make this life of clean countertops, mail stacked neatly in one pile? The effort of love?

From here, stirring, I can turn and see the main room of the house. One soft green couch in a living room, one tidy computer station, one dining room table covered in a bright Mexican tablecloth. Fossils and rocks lined up on the windowsills. Walls occasionally adorned with what must be Amber's earlier-kid artwork. A lemon tree growing in the corner. Plastic boxes stacked in the pantry: LIP BALM SUPPLIES, HONEY EQUIPMENT, SOAP SUPPLIES. There are sprigs of lavender about, bunches of dried wildflowers. Near my feet on the gray smooth floor are metal dogfood bowls that are clean, lined up side-by-side, and if ever there was a sign of you-have-your-shit-together, it's the state of the dogbowls.

I put the batter into a pan, put the pan into the heated oven, find a broom, and gather up the bits of flour and cracker that have scattered. Heartsweeper. Sweeping up my own heart, sweeping up my own body, sweeping up the dusty corners and irregularities. *May I audition for the part,* some song goes. *Of sweeping up your dusty heart? I know your darkest corners fairly well.* I find the trash and let the fine bits of bonewhite fall into the bin.

With the broom, I go to the bathroom and sweep up my tangles of cut hair. They look like long grapevines, twisted into various formations. With dustpan in one hand and broom in the other, I stand and look in the mirror again, startled by my short haircut and how it hangs now that it is dry, the bit of color that has come into my cheeks. I lift my mouth in a small smile just to give it a try. *Feral gone domestic.* I cross my arms to hug myself, fingers touching shirt but stroking curved bone, and regard, gingerly, this person in front of me.

*

The breeze shifts my hair back and forth across my face, making it lift and dance. I've never had hair short enough to be flung about in such a way. The sensation is new. Small, yes, but new, and all any of us has ever hoped for, I think, is to be amazed.

The cake is baking, the kitchen has been tidied, so I close my eyes and lean back against the house. I tilt my head to the sun, the red coloring the back of my eyelids. It smells of dried grasses, like rotting apples, like yellow leaves on the cottonwoods, and, somewhere in the far distance, the sultry sting of a fire. Someone burning out a ditch, no doubt, or getting rid of trash in the burn barrel. My tongue feels out the gap of missing tooth, and the gap feels like wet tissue with bone underneath, which I guess is exactly what it is, a hole that seems to go forever—my tongue can't even find the end of it. The teeth to either side seem surprised, suddenly, to find themselves alone, without their companion; the sides feel new and unexposed, not yet hardened to life. The pus pocket feels the size of an eraser, tough enough to resist the push of my tongue. I assume it will open, the infection will clear. I stab it with a fingernail to see if I can pop it open, but the sting is too great. I scan the rest of my body. My crotch itches: yeast infection for sure. Blood that won't quite stop on top of that. I cough my old cough, and my ribs ache in response. The skin on my cheekbone tightens and dries. The bump on my forehead throbs. My skin is starting to feel sunburned. And my heart keeps beating. Ouch-ouch-ouch drumbeat. But also a here-you-are. Here-you-are.

I open my eyes and pick up a pebble and throw it across the yard, and this makes me look at my silver thumb ring. Slade gave it to me, his version of a wedding band, since that's all I would accept. The sun catches it and sends a sharp slice of light into my eye, so I look the other way, toward the donkeys who are standing nose-to-nose. Blink away the tears. I opened my heart exactly twice. To Slade and to Alejandra. This sense of my heart squeezing itself is the emotion called *regret*.

Next to me is a bike leaning up against the house. Amber's, must be. I wish I missed her. I wish I had missed her in the last ten years, and I wish I missed her now. But I don't know her, and there's nothing *to* miss. I have none of that knowledge. How, for instance, Libby must have got her to this almost-big-bike stage. How years ago, Libby must have run alongside a smaller bike, yelling encouragement, judging the moment of that release, and how some smaller version of Amber, thin-straight-hair-ponytail flying, gained momentum, wobbling, wobbling, then holding steady and smiling. It's only when you've seen something like that that you can feel a hearttwist.

But that is what I am here for. To tell Amber that my departure was never her fault. Thank Libby and Ed. Say goodbye to Kay, I suppose. Write a note to Slade. And to Alejandra. To witness some details, and let them witness a few of mine. Also, I wouldn't mind sleeping out under the stars one last time. I wouldn't mind trying to share a few things about myself. I twist a bit of my hair and gaze off into the distance at the mountains. I wouldn't mind trying to be brave for a few days and trying to sweep up a bit of the mess.

*

Ed drives up in the green Harvester, leans out his window, and regards me. "You doing okay?"

I nod.

"I'm having a bit of trouble with some farm work, actually. I wanted to pull in and double-check on you, but if you're fine, I gotta go."

I nod again, but because he is waiting for more, and deserves it, I say, "I showered and I slept and I ate some and I'm resting. I threw away my clothes in the burn barrel and cleaned up my mess. I was hoping to see Amber when she's off school. In your presence, of course. I'll be polite and kind. I'll leave if she wants me to."

Something soft crosses his face. "You look better," he says. "A lot better. I'll be back in a half hour when Amber gets off the bus. Okay? I'll call Libby and tell her you're still around." He puts the truck into drive and pulls slowly out, glancing in his rearview mirror at me as he goes.

I remember one of the last times I saw him, when my stomach was huge and the baby was hooking her little toes under my lower rib and pushing, right before she'd turned, and right before I gave birth, and I'd gone into Ideal Foods to get some licorice and he was in there too, buying fruit, and we chatted for a moment. I barely knew him, only that he was the newly arrived hippie guy with the orange VW bus who was always talking philosophy in strange loopy sentences, the guy who sometimes walked with a strange gait, like he was skipping, and his hands dancing like a bird having some fun in the sky. He was more fragile then, somehow. Not firmed up. Not yet a man. But maybe on the verge, because I remember that day at the grocery store, he stood with me in the checkout line and told me that he wanted a Wordsworthian life, plain living and high thinking. I told him I wanted High Living and Plain Dying. He had chuckled and said, "Well, Tess, I hope that works out for you."

LISTEN (says one part of Tess's mind): Quit with this. Chin up.

LISTEN (says another): Dying is part of living. High Living and Plain Dying is what you wanted.

LISTEN (says another): Stop shaking, Tess. Bear up. For three days, do this thing.

Tess cries. She doesn't exactly want to go but also sees no other way out, and at least she has the sense to do it right.

No moldering corpse or bloody mess.
Alone. Plain bones.
East of here.
The universe doesn't care about us,
but we care about each other
and ourselves
and the whole enterprise of life,
especially at the moment of death.
When Death approaches,
it clarifies that need for a burst of caring at
the very end.

I take a big breath, dig my fingernails into my wrist, hard enough to streak pain, the pain strong enough to bring me back to my body. *Good girl*. It's just this: I never asked to suffer. I never meant to make other people suffer either. It wasn't *my fault* that I was born. So, no, god. You don't get to judge me for this. I don't forgive *you*.

Chapter Five

The heat is squawking now, an infant's wail demanding that the clouds boiling up in the west sweep themselves across the sky. I look to the white blooms above the mountains to see their response. The clouds are reluctant, tired. They refuse. They want the earth to parch. Close up, though, a fluff of milkweed releases from its pod, over by the fence. The smooth white silk of it rises up, rests, and then is picked up in a gust of wind and sent into the pasture.

I am thirsty and hazy and sunsoaked and sunburned and dozing off when Ed pulls up again. He gets out of his truck and regards me silently while Ringo jumps from the truck, runs to nose me, and then runs back to him. Ed is not like the clouds. He is sure of himself. Direct. Here with a purpose. And sure enough, he walks over to a faucet hooked to a green hose and turns it on. I see the green hose jerk up, filled with water. He walks alongside it until he finds the end, which is at the base of a young apple tree, and now that I'm looking for them, I can see the pattern of newly planted fruit trees, too young to bear fruit but awaiting the possibility.

Ed stares at the hose, then picks it up, the water cascading down near his feet. He drags the hose to another nearby tree, drops it, and walks back up the dirt driveway, away from me. Ringo darts in front of him, tail sweeping bits of sunlight, and lets out a single woof as a yellow bus pulls up, blinking its back-and-forth lights, and the stop sign swings out at the same time my throat constricts. Hilarious, that. A stop sign in the middle of nowhere. A grown heart terrified of a child.

I get to my hands and knees and stand up, slowly, to make sure the world is steady. The shower and cakebaking and sunsleeping have fragiled me—somehow I am less sturdy than I was this morning—and yet I must and will stand for this moment.

I watch Amber get off the bus, cross the dirt road, walk up to Ed. Turquoise T-shirt with a turquoise sweatshirt tied around her waist, bright red backpack, cascade of fine brown hair. Ringo circles her with joy, jabs her with his nose for a pet, circles again. Above her, I see the contrail of an airplane coming toward us, and I wish I'd been in one at least once, how wonderful to fly over strange moments like this.

Ed embraces Amber, waves to the bus driver, points to me, says something. As the bus pulls away, Amber starts walking. Looks up at Ed, asks a question. Stops again. Looks at me. Starts. Reaches down to pet Ringo, who is still circling her legs. The contrail starts to dissipate in the sky as she nears.

She stops to regard me fully for the first time. Her body sways back with surprise—I see her do it—and I'm doing it too. Heartcrunch. We've never seen how much we look alike. It is a new fact for the both of us. I feel my mouth open, hear my intake of a sharp breath.

"You're Tess." She walks straight up to me but stops before she gets too close. Ed stops behind her, clears his throat, puts his hand on her shoulder. I can tell he's looking at me hard, but I keep my eyes on hers.

"You're Tess," she says again.

"Yes." I make a small arc with my hand. "You're Amber."

She looks me up and down, fingers her silver stud earring. She's got a round kid face with those adult teeth like ten-year-olds have, but she's pretty, with paler skin than me, but darker than her father, Simon, who in certain ways was so light and blond that he was like straw. She's tall for her age, with a little round tummy and no sign of hips or breasts yet, although, yes, she's wearing a thick shirt, which means the start of the coverup. Her eyes are beautiful. Almond shaped and dark liquid brown, and the glow of them will be her defining feature, the one that every boyfriend she's ever with will comment on, the one that will cause guys at bars to say, *Wow, you got some eyes there*. She's got my hair, which is a shade darker and a grade finer than Libby's. We stare at each other, and bygod, surely this similarity is in appearances only. She is not me. She will be the opposite of me.

"You were standing outside of school this morning."

"Yes."

"I saw my mom look at you."

"Yes."

"My dad says she knows you're here. That it's okay with her that I talk to you." Her face is open and yet solid, matter-of-fact.

"Yes."

"You look like the photos. Except skinnier and with short hair. We really do look a lot like each other, don't we?"

I make my eyes hold hers, but hers shift above my head, and I turn to see what she's looking at, which is a hawk circling on a current. I clear my throat. "We do, don't we? I didn't realize. You don't look like your father."

"Simon?"

"Yes, Simon."

"Who you had a one-night stand with?"

"It was a brief relationship. Don't you do that."

"He died in a rodeo accident, you know."

"I heard."

"I wasn't sad. I barely knew him."

"I hardly knew him either." It's a rapid-fire exchange, no space in between the words, and finally there is a pause long enough that we can regard each other once again. She's biting her top lip in, and furrowing her brow, which makes her nose crunch. Her eyelashes are crazy-ass long, and she has peach-fuzz hair along her hairline and at the bend of her jaw, just like I do, and I wonder if I'm still a little bit high somehow because all these details sing out at me and my eyes can't unfocus from her face.

She inhales to start the next fast barrage. "Libby's my real mom, you know. You're not."

"Oh boy, I know it." My hands want to reach out, but instead I hold one wrist with one hand and place them against my belly. "I'm not here to argue that fact."

"I'm not going to pretend to know you." Her face grows a little harder. "I've seen pictures of you, but you've never seen me. That's a big difference between us."

"True enough."

"My dad warned me about your cheek. That it's puffy."

"I got a tooth pulled the other day."

"That's what he said. But otherwise, you don't look as bad as he said you did. The way he described you, I thought you might look like a zombie." She shifts the backpack on her shoulder. "Well, that means something, you know. The fact that I know what you look like. But you didn't know about me. You didn't care enough to send an address so we could send you a picture of me. I did keep an extra of all my school pictures, in case you want them."

I rub my hands over my arms, feel the prickles on my skin. "I do want the photos. Thank you."

"You must be pretty mean." She bites her lip and scrunches up her nose again. "I guess I'm glad you're here, though."

"You are?"

"I'm not saying I *like* you. But I'm glad you're here, if only because I've wondered. *Of course* I am curious. Anyone would be curious. Anyway, why?"

"Why what?"

"Why are you here?" But with that, she walks past me, into the house. I open the screen door, and I follow her in after glancing at Ed and seeing him shrug and nod. She stops, lets her backpack slide on the floor with a thump. Ringo sniffs it and runs to his bowl to lap up water. Ed follows us in but stays at the threshold of the door.

"I need to take something out of the oven," I say. "I think it's a cake, but it might not be. Maybe it will be more like a large cookie."

She eyes the golden circle as I take it out with mitts and upside-down it on a plate. She looks at it, worried, and then up at me. "It looks like a very fat pancake. It looks like some geographical formation you might find in Australia or something."

I bark out a little laugh. She gets out the milk and a glass, pours herself some, considers, pours me a glass too. It's only then, while she's holding the heavy jug, I see that her hands are shaking. She's as scared as I am.

At the door, Ed clears his throat. "You want me to come in, honey? Or else I can go unload the bee boxes."

"Do you want some milk, Dad? Some . . . cake?"

"No, but thank you. Later. I'll be right outside. You okay? Just tell me if you want me to make her leave. Or I can come in. You get to pick."

She hesitates. "I'm okay. Take care of the bees." She cuts herself a slice of the flat cake, feeds a crumb of it to Ringo, smiles at Ed. Then she squares her shoulders, turns to face me, and we stare at each other until we hear the slam of the screen door as Ed leaves. He looks back at us, and I can see that he'll be within earshot and plans on keeping it that way.

"The cake didn't fluff up." I poke it with my finger. "It doesn't have enough air." I look at her straight on. "Okay, I'm going to try to be honest. Why am I here? Well, thank you for asking, actually. I wanted to see you, Amber. I regret not . . . oh, about a million things. Not sending you birthday cards. I should have. I'm sorry about not living my life better. I want to say all the things you would expect. Clichés are sometimes clichés for a reason, you know? Because they're true. Anyway. It sounds cliché, but I want to say . . . that I'm very sorry. I hope you know that I didn't leave because of you personally. That is so true. I left because that was always my plan, always always always, and then I got pregnant. This place has been a bad match for me since I was a kid. I never wanted kids. Believe me, I would have been a shitty mom. Probably the shittiest mom ever to exist on the planet, and I knew it, and so I left. And then I just cut that part of my life off. Which is why I didn't send cards or anything. It just didn't *exist*. I have always joked that I was born without emotions. I'm not sure that's my fault. Probably it is. But certainly it isn't your fault. And yet you've had to live with the consequences of it. And for that I am sorry." I take a breath and exhale. That's more or less how I practiced, and it is exactly the truth.

She takes a forkful, considers it for long enough that I know she's trying to calm emotions or form words. "That's what my mom says, that you would have been a bad mother," she says at last.

"I knew Libby would make a better mother. At least I left you with a good woman." I stab the fork into the golden fluff, lift out a forkful, put it on the right side of my mouth. "You okay? I'm not so okay. I feel nervous."

Amber runs her fingers along the edge of her nose, not because of an itch, but because it's her way of manifesting a thought.

"So you're in fifth grade. And Libby is a nurse?"

"She's a real nurse now. Just recently. She was a nurse's aide for a long time, but then she spent two years driving to Denver for classes. She works at the assisted care place. The only one around here."

"Amber? Can I hug you? Just a quick hug?"

She gives a shrug and nods, and so I go up and hold her to me. She smells like honey and feels about as hollow as a bird. I close my eyes and duck my head enough that I can press my scraped cheek against her soft brown hair. It's softer than mine, even. I hold this moment, hugging this younger me that still has a chance. Like me, she's got a small tremor going through her, and I do feel a pang of sorrow that I'm causing this kid confusion and hurt. A new theory goes flying into my head: A person's best chance of forgiveness rests with a child, perhaps, but no one should take advantage of that fact.

She backs away from me before I'm ready, and we stand in an unwieldy silence. "Do you want to talk? Tell me about your life?" I clear my throat and start again. This is so hard for me, to keep words going. "Or do homework? Or what do you normally do now? Maybe I could help you with it. No stress, though. I don't want to stress you out. Whatever you want to do. I'm cool. This doesn't have to be some big huge traumatic conversation. Although, at the same time, it seems important. So, I'm just trying to . . ." But my words have run out; I have nothing more to say.

She stares at me, blinks. "I have chores. Then I relax. Then I do homework. That's what I usually do when I get off the bus. Usually Dad or Mom is here, but this is the first year that I can be left alone now, I'm old enough. For a little bit."

"Does that scare you? To be left alone?"

She pauses. "Sometimes. The house makes weird noises. But I have Ringo."

"Kay used to leave us alone. All the time."

"I know. Mom told me. Kay was an alcoholic. Is an alcoholic." She unclasps a barrette and twists a bit of brown hair in her finger and then resets the barrette and snaps it. I remember Libby playing with my hair. Braids and twists and strange, random creations. I remember how I felt like a cat, purring, whenever she touched my scalp, that I thought it was one of the best feelings in the world. And Libby loved it because my hair was softer, finer, and since she couldn't have it, she said, at least she could play with it. "Mom says that when kids are abused, that they grow up to be adults who think, well, that somehow love is mixed up with hurt. So they keep looking for people who hurt them. Or ways to be hurt. So that they feel alive."

I touch my cheek, smile to myself. "I guess your mom tells you a lot, huh?"

Her eyes shift away from me, her gaze locks on the mountains outside the kitchen window. "Ten-year-olds know about as much as grown-ups. Sometimes they just don't have the experience or the words. My mom thinks it's best to speak the truth, if at all possible. She says that you got messed up by Kay. That you drank a lot of alcohol and then did drugs and then sold drugs. And it's all because—"

"Yeah, yeah, it's always the mom's fault."

She sucks in her cheek. "Well, sometimes it is." Then she reaches out and touches my arm. Maybe to see if I'm real. "Kay was mean to you. Very mean. She's an okay grandma, though. She can be grumpy, but she's got good parts too."

"She's improved?"

"She's calmed down. That's what my mom says."

"She still living with Baxter?"

She considers this. Bites on her lip and twitches her nose, and I realize that that's a tic of hers. Leans on the kitchen counter. After a bit, she says, "My parents didn't tell you anything?"

"No. We didn't have that much time to talk."

She puts down her fork, drinks some milk, wipes her forearm across her mouth. I really did forget what it's like to have those big front teeth that don't quite fit your face. But she's going to be beautiful; I was beautiful, I really was, and she looks like a softer version of me.

"Baxter died. Or *passed*, if you want me to say it that way. About a year ago." Here she stops to look at me, and I realize that she's probably thinking the exact same thing I am, trying to gauge how human I am. Does this news hurt or not?

"Oh, okay." I put down my plate, pick it up, put it down again. "I didn't know that." For her benefit, I add, "Good ol' Baxter." I touch my heart and tap it. "He was a nut. A real nut. He sort of raised us. When Kay was on a binge or just not doing a very good job of it all. Well, I'm sorry to hear that."

Amber examines her hand and then fingers it, running the tip of her finger down each rise of bone. A tear lands on the back of her hand, which she rubs in as well. "I miss him a lot. He was so nice to me. He left his ranch to that place . . . The Nature Conservancy. But Kay has the house and a few acres. She likes living there. She's sick, though   "

Tess smiles, watches herself as if from above,

zooming up to see her own self from different perspectives.

Right now, Tess notices that Tess feels like a dog,

thrusting its nose into someone's crotch.

Not wanting to lose potential love or attention.

Tess used to feel the same way about Baxter.

Wanting to hold his kind attention.

She never told him that, never told him goodbye.

I dig my fingernails into my wrist. "Sick with what?"

She scans the house, as if scanning her brain for the right words. "She stepped on a board with nails in it, and one went almost clear through her foot. This was last year. When she went in, it was all infected. So she was on antibiotics. And she would have been fine. But then she went into the river. She was fishing, and she waded in."

"The Arkansas?"

"Yes."

"What's wrong with walking in the river? I used to all the time."

"Well, she got these bumps on her leg. And that's called staph."

"Oh, boy. I know about staph."

"Not this kind of staph. It's new. It's like that kind you get in hospitals, but worse."

"Is that true? A new strain?"

"Yes." She looks at her feet, as if they might be contaminated. "It's the kind that antibiotics don't work on. So she was in the hospital in Denver for a long time. Getting drugs through her arm. I got to go to Denver. I saw the botanic gardens and the art museum and the mint, where they make money."

I have a sudden vacuum of a realization. All these places are places I took Alejandra to when she was about this age. My other daughter, the one I chose to bring into my life. I recover from the recoil and glance back at Amber. "So why is she still sick, then? After all that?"

"The staph keeps coming back. It won't . . . it just won't die."

"And she's home now?"

"She lives in Baxter's old house. She's ready to die now. She won't go back to the hospital. She's got a bunch of big ugly sores. It's probably the grossest thing you'll ever see. Either Mom or Dad goes over there every morning and every night, to hook up the antibiotics to the IV. My mom scrapes off her skin once a week." She takes a bit of cake and then regards it and takes another bite. "It tastes okay if you pretend it's not supposed to be cake. If you just tell yourself that it's some French dessert you never heard of, then you can enjoy it."

A laugh dripfaucets out of me. "You're funny."

"My parents say it's all in your perception of a thing. If I don't perceive it as cake, it's good. If I perceive you as a new acquaintance, and not a mother, then I can be friendly and suspicious of you at the same time. Which is appropriate."

I reach out to touch her arm. "Clearly, you are very smart. You're already better set for the world than I ever was." I don't say: this is exactly what I wanted to know.

Amber considers this. "But that doesn't for sure make me a good person. The trick is to be both smart and kind." She digs out a piece of cake from her tooth with her tongue. "Let's sit at the table."

We sit, and I trace the pattern of the bright tablecloth with my finger. A zigzag of red, a line of blue. "I don't know where you got your brains from. Not Simon. Not me."

"My mom has always said you *were* smart. She says you were always inventing words and also coming up with theories on life, that you liked to look at big brushstrokes. Those are her words. She said that you couldn't ever be shallow, but you wanted to be. You could see big-picture stuff. You could be fierce. That's a simple fact. You just didn't *care*."

I eat more of the not-cake. It's more like a flat white honey biscuit, and some of it gets stuck in the missing-tooth gap, which stings, but my tongue cleans it out, runs itself gently over the hurt. "Amber, I don't know how you feel about me being here. I feel like you're being very brave. I feel like you're being very generous. Thank you. But if you don't want to be, well, I'll leave if you want. You're the boss right now. But I'd like to stay and hang out for a bit."

She headtilts and regards me. "How long?"

"How long will I stay?" I give her a calm look, which is a lie, a coverup for all the lightning going on underneath. "A coupla days?"

Tess's STUPID FUCKING nerves
attacking her again at random:
throat closing up,
pounding heart,
dry mouth
can't breathe.

I pop my neck and think: It depends, Amber. It depends on you. Because a gal can only be strong for so long, and sometimes she just needs to be saved. By someone who cares. Libby, for instance, the one person who helped. She helped in little ways while I grew up. She helped in big ways, by taking my daughter so I could get the hell out of here. So, you see, I'm asking for help without deserving it. And if you say *no*, well, then I have my Last Resort card in my back pocket.

"There are no extra rooms here," she says, and then, because I'm spacing out, she says it again.

"Okay." But I'm thinking: Do you see, Amber? It's my Last Resort backpocket card that keeps me trudging on in life, and coming home was the last thing I needed to do before I could play it. But now that it's down to the wire, I find that I'm scared. Afraid to pull it, afraid to play it.

"And I don't want to share my bedroom."

"Okay. I totally get that."

"Maybe you could stay with Kay?"

"Maybe."

We both startle when a treebranch hits the roof. The wind is picking up. Her eyebrows suddenly furrow, and she stands. "Do you smell smoke? No one should be burning ditches."

I follow her outside the door, and we scan the horizon, our eyes squinted against the wind. There are dry grasslands to the north and to the east, a field of milo to the south, and the dim outline of mountains in the far distance to the west, the haze of the brown cloud that hangs in the atmosphere from all the pollution from the Front Range.

Tess sometimes thinks:

You may not be clued in to the earth

But the earth is clued in to you.

I take a few steps away from the house so I can see the horizon. "It feels like a hundred degrees out here. It's always been too hot here on the plains. That's why I like the mountains." I look off to them, which is where the sun is hanging. "And the angle of the sun. It's so hard this time of year. It's always in your eyes. It smells like someone is burning out a ditch, or burning trash in a burn barrel."

Tess's body grows quiet

and the world does too.

Tess knows this feeling.

It's when the universe is trying to tell her something,

and she needs to hold still and listen.

"Oh, wow," I say, my brain making vague connections. "I heard on the radio earlier in the day, when I was making that cake, there's a wildfire in the mountains. *That's* what we smell. That's why it's so hazy."

"We can smell a wildfire in the mountains from here?"

"Yes. I think that's it."

"But it's so far away."

"Well, it's a pretty big fire. That's where I used to live. Those mountains. The haze is going to make the sunset so pretty, so red. All the particles in the air. What a mess. Colorado, I mean. Every year now, it burns."

She turns to face the blue outline of mountains. "But it won't get to us."

I look at her, touch her shoulder. "Oh, no, that's impossible. It's very far away. But the smoke travels on windy days. See how the wind is coming straight from the west?"

"I want to do my chores." She walks across the driveway to a cement water tank, turns it on, bends over to watch the water burble through the hose and into the cement rectangle. That reminds me of Ed's fruit trees, and I turn to see him moving the water on them again and then turning to watch the mountains himself.

Once the water is going, Amber turns around and stares at me, as if I'm supposed to walk over there too. So I do. When I come up from behind her, she points to the cows that are wandering slowly toward us.

Their knees look like huge knots in a tree. "This is Franny and Zooey," she says, nodding to the cows. "These cows both had calves this spring. But it's fall now, and we need to wean and sell them. The other ones we're keeping, though. For milk."

I stare at the cow that comes forward to get a scratch from Amber. The other cow dips her nose into the tank, raises it, nuzzles the first with a nose still trickling water, and then head-butts the first cow out of the way for her own scratch. As I watch Amber laugh and lean forward so that she can reach the other, I start humming.

Humming because I am now out of words, of strength, worn down from meeting my daughter, and I'm just now seeing that perhaps I shouldn't have come at all—it's too hard once a heart has been met by another. I also wonder at Amber's willingness to speak to me at all, wonder if it comes from shock—it's too hard to be gruff and angry when you're not prepared. I stop humming, clear my throat. Still, I must try. I hug my arms to my chest. "Was that hard, in earlier years? Selling the calves?"

She eyes the mountains. "Wow, look at the sky. It's turning red. That's gonna be the prettiest sunset ever." She looks at me, surprised, as if I'm the one responsible for it, and then adds, "Well, weaning calves, it's part of life."

"True enough. Every living thing in this world gets weaned eventually. Right?"

She considers that. "Maybe not humans."

"You don't think so?"

"Naw. Even my mom needs to know her mom is okay." She turns to consider me and then looks back at the setting sun, a bright red globe hanging over the mountains and sending sprawling oranges and reds spiking in all directions and lighting up the few clouds that are above us in a deeporange glow. "Maybe some humans don't need their mamas. But most do."

PART II

Water

Chapter Six

People regularly ask forgiveness for the sins they commit, but they often don't ask forgiveness for the things they neglected to do. But those are sins too. Perhaps they are the greatest sins of all.

*

Redemption is found in the most unusual of activities, and so when Amber says her homework is something she can handle *easily, on my own* (which means *I need a moment to myself*), I go to the kitchen to make a salad.

Redemption is found in love, and if you want to know if you're a loving person, ask the person you're with if they feel loved.

Redemption is found in remembrance. I remember Alejandra. She was far off in the distance when I first saw her, a broad brush-stroke of *humanchild* in the middle of *hugedesert*. (Like Amber, a backpack on her shoulders. Unlike Amber, she was standing alone when I first saw her, alone in a verystill verydangerous world.) When I parked the pickup and walked toward her, I could see the basic situation: a group of humans huddled under the branches of a mesquite tree. They'd snapped off creosote branches and were huddled below them, to make a canopy, to conceal, to console, and I was thinking of how similar it was to a rattlesnake, curling around sage in order to stay cool.

All the faces turned to me, and there was a small burst of energy: to determine if I was friend or foe, although they hardly had the energy to care. This girl whistled and, when I got closer, called out to me, "*Hola, güerita bonita.*" As if she had already determined that I was good, beautiful, worth loving.

I stood there, staring at her. It took me a moment to understand that they had arrived sooner than I'd been told, that their milk jugs of water were empty, that they had been waiting and waiting for me. As I got closer, I could smell them, the blood and stink and perhaps even burnt flesh. I could see their blistered lips, ripped shoes, dead-eyes. I could see the coming of hyperthermia, dehydration. Their story, which came in fragments, was similar to every other story I'd heard, but unique in the particulars of their souls. All from Chiapas, all going to Denver to meet cousins. To work on tennis courts. They'd been told that the walk was only a day or two and that two gallons of water each would suffice. A *coyote* lie. They'd been told I'd be there two days ago.

The kid, Alejandra, was squatting over the woman who I later learned was her mother, Lupe. Alejandra's black hair was caught in knots and greasy enough to hold the dirt. Blisters all over her mouth, a bloody scrape that ran alongside her face. She kept saying, "*Mamá, la levantona está aquí! Es una gringa! Una güerita bien bonita!*" She kept licking her lips so that she could smile, completely oblivious to how horrible and beautiful she looked. She kept smiling at me as if I were something special, and the others looked at her as if *she* were special. Clearly, she'd been given the most water, the last of the food.

I got water and food and slowly helped them to the truck, one by one, even the men leaning on me, all of us stumbling around, tripping over the bush and the yucca and the prickling floor of the desert, past the empty milk jugs, abandoned clothing, past the sign proclaiming *No más cruces en la frontera*. We walked as if we were drunk. Piss and blood and dirt and grime. Gagging with the smell of animal, with heat. Finally, the men were able to settle in the back of the horsetrailer—*gracias gracias*, they kept murmuring—their throats too swollen to make it sound like anything but a blur. Their toes swollen and rotten when they pulled off their shoes.

I put Lupe and Alejandra up in the cab with me, though it was not protocol and would have sent Slade into a frenzy. But I didn't care. I was too carefree to care. I wanted them to have air conditioning and comfort. If any vehicle came into sight, they were to crawl under a blanket. Risky, but I felt like a god. Better than a god, because I was trying to temper their suffering.

They were so grateful for water. They had tears for the crackers, moans at the bananas. Ointments and tortillas and pillows. And that girl, her fingers always roaming over her mother, and after the initial recovery of drowsy sleep, always chattering, asking me questions, translating for her mom in solid English interspersed with awkward sentences.

That was five years ago. Then something else happened, and that's the last moment I remember of my old self, the one that was seamless, the one who was just me, just Tess, united. That's when I began to hear a voice speaking to me. A voice that spoke to me of forgiveness and redemption. It wasn't my voice, exactly. It wasn't anyone else's voice, either. It was the broken voice of the universe, and I was finally sunk enough to tune in and listen.

*

From the kitchen window, I see that the sun has sunk to its low-down setting position, and the sky lights up in one last fling of red-orange glow. I shake my head to let the memory go, then I slam my palm on the counter to make my brain listen. I cradle my stinging palm in my other hand and then turn the radio dial again until I get the crackly NPR station, which has finally decided to air the news. Wildfire, as per usual: *Type I fire. White Wolf Fire. Trailers, communication units, hotshot crews, heli-tankers. Wild-urban land interface. The fire is burning a little bit of everything, but not all of anything. The burn line goes up and down canyons, through houses and around houses.* Always reported with such surprise, though Colorado has been burning for years now. I've been through the remains of enough of them to cease being surprised. The burned skeletons of old trees. The emerald green grasses of spring. The baby aspen trees poking up through charred soil. The waves and waves of blackened trees in the far distance.

Ed crosses my line of sight. He's moving from one shed to another with large white buckets in his hands. Feeding the cows or chickens or donkeys, I suppose. A bit later, he moves again, carrying white boxes into an outbuilding, and although I think they are bee boxes, he's not even wearing one of those goofy bee suits.

We can't figure out where the fire line is, because it's everywhere. Perimeter crews. One homeowner missing.

I push jars around in the cupboard. Wheat germ and jars of home-made rosehip tea and homemade pickles. Surely, some alcohol around here somewhere! Finally, behind the bag of coffee in a cupboard, I find a bottle of Seagram's 7, full up to the neck. What a pretty color, both in the bottle and as it faucets down into a coffeecup. What a pretty smell. What a pretty taste.

All residents encouraged to evacuate. It's the most difficult conditions here. Leave your homes. Winds are changing direction.

Ed appears again, water buckets now hanging from his arms.

Ringo follows in a roundabout way, guided into figure eights and in crisscross patterns by his sniffing nose—imagine people crossing the desert like that. They'd die before they got a half mile. He pounces on some imaginary mouse, runs in happy circles.

Immigrants not located. We now believe that an immigrant started the fire, as a signal fire. (Huh. Stupid, stupid. I wonder whose run that was.)

Ed has stopped midway and is glancing toward me, at the window, and then toward the mountains, as if he, too, is considering the source of the smoke. He shakes his head to himself.

"Is that the fire we smell?" Amber is suddenly behind me, leaning against the wall.

"Yes, I think so." I put my coffee cup on the counter, though I can see she's noticed it. I turn my attention back to cutting the gnarled and curved carrots.

"It sounds bad." Amber walks into the kitchen and leans against the fridge. "Remember that about a month ago, there were four different fires going? I'm glad we don't live in the mountains after all. I used to want to live there. But not now."

"Yes. I heard about those. It's been a bad summer. Winter is coming, though, and that might make it better."

"The fire won't get here. You said it wouldn't."

"No, it won't get here." I move the carrot chunks to the side of the cutting board with my knife and then pick up a tomato. "Hey, Amber? Where's White Wolf Canyon? I never heard of that one. Could you do a search for me? Which part of Colorado is burning? I'm just curious."

> Tess's heart is pounding or quitting
> or she doesn't know what,
> and she grabs on to the kitchen counter, and the room
> spins, and her heart spins, and the universe spins.
> She needs Amber out of the room.

She disappears and after a pause yells, "Near Alamosa. That's in the southern part of the state, they say. It looks pretty, on the images. The mountains, I mean. They're big. They go on forever."

"Did they say when it started?" I keep my voice steady.

Pause. "Yesterday."

"That many acres in one day? That's impossible."

Amber comes into the kitchen. "The wind, they say. The wind gusts are super bad. I'm glad you're not in the mountains, that you came to visit us now." Those almond-shaped deep brown eyes have the smallest lines of green near the pupil. Just like mine. But the green is like flecks of fishscale, flecks of mica, flecks of lifegreen. "That would be scary, wouldn't it? To be there now? You okay?" Amber whispers it, with real concern.

"Oh, maybe. It's because your eyes are so pretty," I whisper, calm, fading out. "They're so beautiful, Amber. *You* are so beautiful."

"Thank you." Shrug. But she's smiling. It meant something. She feels seen. Then she adds, "Tess? Are you really all right?"

I lean against the counter to brace myself. "Amber, can I say one thing?" Still my voice is quiet, a calmness enforced by the universe, a solidness pushed into me by some outside force. I clear my throat. "When you walk behind a horse, you're supposed to walk *right* behind the horse. As you know. Because if you step back a bit, and that horse kicks, it has more power, more momentum, and he's gonna get you good. You need to get *way* behind the horse, or stay up close."

"I know. Kay taught me. Baxter too."

"Yes. Life is like that. Move *toward* danger. It's safer that way. Either that, or get the hell out of the way." I pause. Try to look brighter, more alive. "Not that you are in the mood to be taking any advice from me. For sure. But I learned something from leaving you." And here, I take my hand off the counter and put it over my eyes so I can have the dark. My voice goes soft again and not even really of my own accord. I just hear it, with a bit of surprise. "To me, Amber, you were a danger. Your infant self. Because you represented everything I didn't want to give up. My freedom, my partying. So I ran off. I got far away from that danger. Which was you. I'm sorry to say. But Libby did the opposite. She looked right at the danger, which was you—because you were also a danger to her—she had no money, no real job, no love, no nothing—and she pulled you in. In *close.*"

I open my eyes to find her staring at me, biting the inside of her upper lip. "Okay." And then, because I look so pleading, she adds, "Either get far away from the danger, or move in really close. That's what you're saying."

"Exactly."

"Okay, Tess."

"Another example. Let's say I'm driving and a deer steps out in the road. If I swerve to miss that deer, if I take a half-assed position, I'm likely to die. I could drive off a cliff or swerve just enough to hit an oncoming car. They'll teach you this in driver's ed. If you must, you go ahead and keep the car straight and hit the deer. You go *at* the danger. Now, if you can stop, and avoid the deer altogether, then great, do that. But do not, ever, ever, ever, put yourself in that land in-between."

She bites her lip again, regards me. "You're softer than I thought you'd be."

A soft, genuine laugh burbles out of me. "Worn down, like a river rock." I don't say: I'm crazyferal and that has made me soft now. I reach out to touch her cheek. "Life is a crazy mix of knowing when to step forward toward danger and when to run as fast as you can."

That's what Tess came here to say.

Oh, Amber.

Please try to watch for the two paths

and pick the right course.

She says something about her homework and reaches out to touch my arm and then wanders off. I put my hands on the counter and lean forward and look out the window toward the mountains. I can't stay now. I'll need to go far away, as far as I can go.

Chapter Seven

As we set the table and pass plates and move food from serving plate
to dinner plates, the silence I keep nearly breaks my eardrums. I must
guide the ship through calmer waters. In this way, we have our main
course, which is to stay the course. Instinct tells us what will not be
discussed. (The running of undocumented immigrants.) (My current
situation.) (Whether I will see Kay.) (What caused the fire.) (What I
should ask to be forgiven for.) Instead, we allow what will be discussed:
"What happened to your tooth?" (Got it pulled by a dentist.) And "Do
you need to see a doctor? For a checkup?" (No, I do not, but thank you.)
And "How was Kay after Baxter?" (He'd helped her improve, so she
handled it better than you might think.) And "She quit drinking?" (She
slowed way down for a while, only took it back up recently.) And "She
gonna die soon?" (Pause. It's possible.)

What nearly lets the sails out, nearly takes me off course, is the
miracle of an honest meal. Not cellophane wrap, not pizza, not chips.
No. Here is steamed broccoli and grilled zucchinis and summer squash
in herbs, salad, wild rice mixed with diced mango, yesterday's leftover
roasted chicken.

The four of us sit at a table with bright plates, bright napkins. Blues, oranges, yellows. The energy feels quietly bright, too: Amber, still in her turquoise sweatshirt, her brown hair pulled back in a pony, nervous but settling. Ed in a clean light purple T-shirt and thoughtful as he looks out the window, at the twilight, considering something. Libby, who came home from work and put on a skyblue dress and who has braided her hair and who looks prettier than she did at eighteen. She glances at me from time to time, whispers something along the lines of "You look better" or "I'm not so worried anymore" or "You just needed sleep and a shower, I think," to which I nod and nod again. From time to time, I speak little phrases, too—"Thank you for letting me sit here and eat with you"—which seems to surprise Libby every time. She looks particularly startled at one moment, in fact, but it's at something out the window, and we turn to see a fox calmly trotting by, barely visible from the leftover light in the sky and the outdoor bulb on a telephone pole.

"That fox doesn't get your chickens?"

Ed chews thoughtfully. "Not yet." Then, "Ringo, go give that fox a scare."

Ringo seems to understand and charges out of the house through a dog door in a bounding woof, but the fox is already gone, and Ringo seems too lazy to take pursuit, and instead sits down to scratch himself in the circle of light.

"Did you know," I say, "that there are about twelve million illegal immigrants in the United States?" I do not say: My pick-up location was called Lobo's Pass, because it was Lobo's favorite spot. White Wolf Creek. But what are the chances?

"Tess?" Ed hands me a plate of vegetables. "Are you okay?"

Blink, blink. "Oh." Crack my neck. Then, "Do you ever feel like everyone is just pretending?"

He pauses, does a little relaxed bob with his head, which means, *Maybe, yes.*

"We're all suckers for a happy ending. Or a happy story in the middle. Go around in our own private movies."

"Sometimes, yes. Why?"

"I was thinking that I never even tried to grow a vegetable." I clear my throat, feel my stomach churn. I thought I had a couple of days, and there is a lot I had hoped to say. I take a big breath. "Did you know that there are whistle languages in rural Mexico? When people need to communicate, and they're far away from each other, and it's too hard to yell? When your voice won't carry? Lots of people use whistles, of course. Hunters. Campers. But this is a whole language." I demonstrate. The whistle of a meadowlark. The whistle of a canyon wren. Some deep whistles, some twittering, flighty ones. "Did you know, for example, that a yell only travels about five hundred feet? But a whistle can travel for nearly ten thousand. No joke. One thing I did learn in my line of work was whistle language. But you don't just whistle. If you need it to travel, you have to use your hands. It's a real trick, a real skill." Here, I put one finger in my mouth, another cupped around my lips, and blow.

They all startle, and Amber jumps in her seat and covers her ears.

"Cripes, Tess," Libby says, scowling. "Please don't shatter our eardrums."

I laugh, do a softer one, this time rolling my tongue, cupping my hands around my mouth. "People have studied these languages. And once, it saved a girl. Can I tell you that story? I'd like to. There was a young girl that I did mother, once." I look at Amber. "I didn't do right by you, Amber. I wasn't here for you. But I just wanted to tell you, I guess, that I was good to a child, once. Would it bother you to hear such a story?"

Amber glances at Libby and then back at me. "No."

"This girl, I suppose she was twelve-ish at the time, and that was about five years ago, well, she simply came to me when I was ready, when I was a bit softer, and a bit more open than when I had you. Her own mother, Lupe, was a good one, but tired, and sometimes it helps to have an extra person who cares." I stare out the window for a moment, at the twilight, at Ringo, who is still resting in the circle of light. "I guess I just wanted to tell you about her. To show you that I had it in me to be kind."

Amber nods, weighing this. "How did you meet her?"

"She was in a group of immigrants I was supposed to pick up in the desert." At this, Ed clears his throat, and Libby starts to say something, and so I quickly add, "Back when I was doing this stuff, which, of course, I should not have been doing."

"I knew you were doing that anyway." Amber glances at Libby. "Kay told me a long time ago. Plus. Well. I'm not stupid. Let her tell the story. Please?"

Libby rolls her eyes at the ceiling but then nods, and so I continue. "She was whistling to me, the loudest whistle I ever heard. Otherwise, I may not have found them, they were concealed so well. I had driven out there in a truck with a horsetrailer. I parked the truck and walked up to them, and I could see right away that they were all tired and . . . well . . . not doing so well. I took the group to Denver, which was what I'd been assigned to do. But unlike every other person I ever drove, I stayed in touch with her. Helped them get on their feet."

I listen to how quiet the room has become, breathe out, determined to try to finish my story. "When I met her, she was so thin, she'd been pounded thin by life, and her hair was so matted and filthy that I couldn't brush it out. She said, 'I'm feeling neargone.' That was her word for it. I had to give her a haircut, just like I did today on me, and that made her cry. But it grew back, and she grew so fast that next year, just shot up. She's back in Mexico, now, with her family. She went back because her grandmother was dying. We've fallen out of touch. I guess that's my fault. Although I did send her packages sometimes, but she quit writing back. People move on to their own lives. Probably she's working or in love . . . it would make me happy to think so, at least."

Amber is smiling softly in a way that makes me think this story isn't hurting her. Perhaps she never expected my love, so it doesn't hurt that it went elsewhere. She waits for more and then finally says, "Is that the end of the story?"

I glance at Libby and Ed. "More or less. It's just that I took good care of her. *I* took *her* to the zoo and the mint. I helped Lupe get a job. I cooked for them sometimes. It's the last time I made a salad, actually. It's the last time I had a home. I know I'm not supposed to talk about this stuff. But I just wanted to tell you about one person. This Alejandra."

Amber puts her elbows on the table, picks them up and straightens up, glances at Libby. "Where have you been sleeping since then?"

I shrug. "Oh, here and there. With friends. In a tent. In a car."

"And where are you gonna sleep tonight?"

I dig my fingernails into my wrist and smile at her. Bless kids for saying what needs to be said. I shrug again, and Libby says, "Tess, you're welcome here. There's only the couch, though. It's probably not long enough for you. There's also a cot out in the shed that we use when one of the horses is foaling or there's a good reason to sleep outside. Kay also has extra rooms. Remember Baxter's old farmhouse? Lots of rooms, lots of beds."

I glance around the table and settle on Amber. I clear my throat, look past them at the twilight outside the window, back at her. "If you don't mind, I have a certain penchant for sleeping outside in the back of pickup trucks. Just a roll or a pad and a sleeping bag? If the mosquitoes and bugs are bad, I sometimes stretch mesh over the top. Could I do that? I'm too tired to see Kay. I'll go in the morning. I sleep really well even with the wind, and the crickets, and the cold.

I like to wake up and look at the sky. Out here, I bet the Milky Way is clear as can be. It's no joke. I really love outside. I know it's odd."

"We've got mosquito netting," Ed says. "I can't say that I blame you."

Libby stretches her neck one way and then the other, just like I do, but she doesn't twist hard enough to make it pop. "We have camping pads. That sounds nice. But Kay. You really need to see her."

"Tomorrow, I'll find my bravery. Thanks for the vegetables. Thank you all for . . . well . . . this." I bow my head in what feels like prayer, pull myself back to my body. How unloved I have been. How unlovable I have been.

> This is the opposite
>
> of what is raging in Tess's heart.
>
> It's simply nice—perhaps a moment of grace—
>
> for Tess to quietly witness the opposite.

It's Amber's sharp voice that brings me back. "Look, hey, look!" I glance up to see her pointing outside.

We all stand up to look out the window. For a moment, there is nothing, and then a soft red glow in the distance—one here and one over there, like someone turning on and off a faraway lamp, the clouds fuzzing and dulling a distant storm. Then a streak of lightning cleaves the sky, a red brighter than any mountainflower, any blood, any fruit. A red that pierces the dark of the eye. We gasp at the same time that the echo and boom hit us, and the thunder rolls as the branches of lightning fade from the main channel. For a moment, then, nothing. Then the whole sky lights, as if daytime has surged into the night, and then the sky goes dark again. One last red bolt flies across the dark sky.

> But wait, Tess thinks.
>
> If Tess's whole life is defined by what she *didn't* do,
>
> then this fire is impossible. Could not be her fault.

Tess's life doesn't have enough substance
to give birth to something like this.

It's like a math problem. If a, then b, therefore c.

If Tess is a) empty, then b) empty,
therefore, c) she could not have caused this.

With Tess, there is *no content*.
You can't sum up zeros.

But no: maybe it's like the lightning.
Two zeros collide in the air,
and they explode.
Create something magnificent and huge,
like a fire,
like a universe.

"It's like tonight's sunset." Amber stands up and moves to the window, touches the pane with a finger. "It's the dust in the air, isn't it? *Relámpago rojo*."

Ed steps to the window and opens it. A rush of cool, noisy, rain-filled wind gusts in, carrying with it the smell of smoke. "Maybe the storm will put out the fire? Or maybe it will start a new one. Hard to know."

"Red lightning. The sky is afire." My voice is quiet, distant, as if I am in another room. I clear my throat. "The channel of the bolt glows red because of the particles in the air. The channel is, you know, basically a gigantic electrical spark. I heard once that red lightning is a hue of which is never seen anywhere else on earth. Only in the sky. It's rare, this red lightning. I've never seen it in the mountains. Only out here on the plains. Such a strange thing . . ."

Amber glances at me and mutters something along the lines of *Libby said you were always reading, always smart.* The sky lights up again, more dully now, and the clouds start to spit rain. Only now am I understanding: the people I could not find set a signal fire to be found, which means they had been starving or dying of thirst. They were there all along, and they were suffering, suffering enough to do one last call for help, and this wildfire is raging because I failed them.

*

Stick to your life like a bur. Stick to your body like a bur. For just a bit longer, Tess. To do that, I focus on the simple motions, which help me stay in my body, especially if I can feel the edge of pain. In washing dishes, for example, how I might run the water a little too hot. Ed is annoyed with me, though, since the plates I'm handing him to dry are steaming, and so he shifts me out of the way and we change positions. His hands are now in soapy water, and I have the towel in my hand.

Amber and Libby are in the other room, mumbling over homework; Ringo is sleeping nearby; and Ed and I shift our weight from one foot to the other, standing at the sink. Outside in the dark, the rain from the storm is now pelting down in wondrous ways—sideways and then lifting and then pouring, lit in the rectangle of the window.

On one plate handover, I see Ed's wrist. One tattoo, a cross. Not right for a gringo like him. It means *I've crossed the border.*

"So, Ed, you gave it up?"

"Give up what?"

"*Levantón*-ing."

He glances at me, back to the dishes. "Yes. The year you left."

"They say you never took any money."

"I didn't."

"Your name was *Salvador.*"

"Yes."

"Why'd you do it in the first place? That's a lot to put on the line." He doesn't answer, so I try again. "Which of the groups did you work with?"

He lowers his voice. "I don't know what you're talking about."

"Oh, Ed. Not only did you do it, you moved here because of it, didn't you? I realized that a few years ago. Colorado is a hub. You picked the best possible place to live. You didn't show up in eastern Colorado by accident. You know there are two major routes, and they both come through here."

"Keep your voice down, Tess." He starts the faucet, rinses, hands me another plate. "This is one thing we don't share with Amber. Although I'm glad you told your story. I'm glad you were kind to someone out there."

"Well, who's helping those people now? I assume they still need a savior."

He hands me a dish. "Not me. I have a child. That's serious stuff with consequences. As you well know. It's gotten so ugly. So dangerous."

"I did it for the money. You did it for, what? Grace? What is it in your life that you needed grace *for*? What did you need forgiveness *from*?"

He hands me a fistful of silverware, a few suds still dripping down the clean edges. "I suppose we both have some stories." He pauses to hand me another handful right as the rain picks up again. "I'm not discussing this with you, Tess."

Like a bur. The sweetstrange earth absorbs the water outside, my sweetstrange time on earth presses me forward. "Ed? I'll sweep and mop. But first I need to tell you something." I pause. I'm no good at this. But I must try to get some words out, to share myself. "Alejandra? Who I mentioned at dinner? I taught her your phone number. Actually, I gave your phone number to several people in case they needed a backup. In case they needed someone. It was somehow consoling to me, to put the burden on you. To use you in that way. I'm sorry. But did any ever . . . call? Did any ever need you? You never heard from Alejandra, did you?"

His eyes shift to something softer. He starts to speak, pauses, starts again. "A few people contacted me over the years. They told me they'd gotten my number from you."

"Did they all end up safe?"

"Yes," he whispers back with a tenderness that surprises me. "Listen, there's something I should tell *you* . . ." But then he shakes his head no, purses his lips.

I wait, but when it's clear he's not going to speak, I brace my hands on the countertop, look at my bare feet on the smooth gray floor. "Ed, I have to tell you something else. The fire . . ."

I look over at him. His sandy-curly hair, his sweet innocent face. "I think . . ."

Clear throat, hold eyes steady.

". . . that group I was supposed to pick up in Alamosa . . . three days ago? I waited three days. I think they were waiting in White Wolf Canyon. I think they were lost and started a signal fire yesterday. I just heard it on the radio. They think the fire was started by a signal fire. In the same location where I was . . ."

The way his brow furrows. Then he turns to me, and his expression changes, fast as a fist flying at me, and I duckfast, throw my elbow up, shove my palm out. Ed darts back, looks confused, holds up his hands, palms out. At the same time he gives me a look that means, *Tess I wasn't going to hit you.* But he whispers: "No. You're lying."

"You guys almost done in there?" Libby's voice. Singsongy.

I watch his face. It has only been a few seconds, but in those seconds, I am seeing him wrecked. "Oh, no. No, no." He flips on the radio, and immediately there is *The fire has increased in size to . . . the winds . . . unstoppable. Again, the worst wildfire in Colorado history . . .*

I cock my head to the boom and echo and then roll of thunder. A rush of words vibrates in my bones and comes boiling out. "It's Colorado. It's fall. It's September. Climate change is not *my* fault. All the trees are dead from beetle kill. It hasn't rained in, like, forever. Right? Right? That's what I'm thinking. And why'd they start a signal fire?" I can feel my voice rising, words pelting faster and faster like the rain. Frantic. "I was there. I was at the location. But let's say we had it mixed up. Let's say I had the GPS coordinates wrong. Let's say they were maybe nearby. It can be surprisingly hard to find water in those mountains. So they started a fire. Probably about the same time I drove away and into Alamosa. And the van I had, for transporting them to Denver, was Lobo's. And I knew I couldn't just take off with it, because then he *would* really be mad, have a reason to come for me. So I left it in Alamosa and slept with a guy to get the Greyhound bus ticket to come here. So while I was coming here, the fire was just starting. Do you see? It was just one moment too late. One moment just slightly off."

Ed's face is still broken, but now he is covering it with his palms, and he makes a long, louder noise that sounds like his throat is constricted. "Oh, Tess." Then he is pacing, one side of the kitchen to the other. Hands flying in silent gestures. "Oh, Tess. Tess. It's you again. You just leave fires in your wake everywhere."

"You guys okay in there?" Libby's voice is chirpy, innocent. It breaks my heart.

"We'll be out in a bit," I singsong at her, because I don't want her in here, don't want to share this news, don't want her to see her husband wildeyed. Lies can be beautiful. I turn to him. I whisper it. "I *didn't know*. Please believe me. I went to pick them up, they weren't there, I left. Simple as that. I didn't know they started a fire. That it spread. Let me spend one more day with Amber. Let me see Kay. Then I'll go. I'll go." Then I add, "They're probably dead, right? The *pollos*? Oh, Jesus,

Ed. Although someone had to survive to tell the authorities it was a signal fire in the first place. I never meant . . ."

He looks at me, still confused, and starts rambling bits of words. His face looks as human as a face can look. No mask, no fake, no solidness. All of it is hitting him: the fact that I did not pick up people, and now they have likely burned, and so have mountains and deer and homes, and all of this is hitting him, and he keeps saying, "But wait, but wait," as if that will help stop the truth.

I keep watching him, unable to take my eyes off of him. I watch him suffer, and all I can think is, *Oh god, not him too, he's just a human. He has to fight hard to not split apart, too.* Behind him, in the square of light, the rain suddenly stops, and the silence that follows sounds as hollow as dried-up bones.

Chapter Eight

The sting of stars. The storm has swept the sky. The stars are spat-
tered by a broad brushstroke, a thick Milky Way that spirals out into
little flecks. One lone burr streakdazzles across the sky. The moon is
full and also glows a bit red. The soft swishing fabric of the sleeping
bag is a louder version of the wind. From the back of the pickup, on my
camping pad, in my sleeping bag, I sit up enough to pour another glass
of whiskey. Raise it to the sky and make a toast:

> To the wildfire, to the mountains,
> to the deer and the moose and the elk and the bears,
> to the fleeing humans who will never be quite the same
> and the ones who died.

> To the soulwrenchers that cascade into a body,
> to the *thump thump thump* of her heart.

> To Tess, who needs to hurry and be ready to go.

To Tess, the spark of a soul, who is outraged to find out that
she can feel.

To the unknown woman in the desert,
a woman and her child who had particular brands of desires
and dreams.

Breathe yourself back in, Tess. So much depends upon a moment.
Amber, Amber, Amber, I want to tell you the rest of the story. I didn't
finish my story.

Here is the rest, Amber: Five years ago, I was driving them all to
Colorado, and the men were in the back of the horsetrailer, and Lupe
and Alejandra were up front. On we went. Eventually I had to pee, so
I pulled over. I could have stopped one moment earlier or later. But I
did not. I stopped right then. There I was, squatting next to the truck,
when I decided this was a good place for a drop, where I could leave
the gallons of water and shoes and blankets, as I often did back then. I
lugged this stuff a quarter mile out from the truck, because if any *pollos* came by, they'd be *near* the road, but not be *on* the road, and they
would find this gift—this offering that I mark with a white cloth on a
stick—of items that they might need.

I was walking along, looking for rattlesnakes, for cactus, for dan-
gers, when I came across something else.

That was the last moment.

Last moment.

The last moment of the Tess I knew, the last moment of my old self.

There, at my feet, was a human skull. Long black hair and a red
barrette. I peered closer. *What the fuck?* I thought. *Wait, what?*

I peered for a long time at the gold cap on one of her teeth. Fascia
holding her ribcage together. A simple fact: a dead woman, not newly
dead, but not there long, either, not yet scattered by bobcats or coyotes.

Oh, Amber, down low, by the pelvis, was an unborn infant. It was curled up, just like in the pictures. It had a huge skull and tiny little fingers and leg bones. Knees bent. Hands curled in. Just like you'd expect. Except the skull was bigger than you'd think, the rest of the bones smaller. A baby ready to be born. A baby never to be born.

It stays on in the mind, you see.

*

I curl up in a fetal position in my sleeping bag, my cocoon, and hold my knees. *No no no don't ever tell Amber that, don't tell anyone that.*

*

I grab my head, dig my fingers into my scalp. But it comes, the details. Tiny handbones scattered. A shoe. I paused and searched for more —*Why? Why did I do that? Why did I look?* The arc of two beautiful arm bones, and then another pile of tiny bones, which must have once made up the other hand. But my eyes drifted back to the baby's skull, right there, perfectly placed in the nest of pelvic bones, waiting for her chance to come into this universe.

What did I do? What have I done? What have I neglected to do? I didn't kill her. But someone did.

(an economy, a nation, a woman wanting work,

a desert,

a drought, a lack of water)

I knelt down and reached my hand into the ribcage. Into the pelvis of this woman. I touched this baby's skull. Wanted to pull it up, wanted to free it from the cavity, get it out in the space between ribcage and pelvis. Even if it meant all the other bones would crumble. I did that. I pulled hard. I freed the skull. I cradled it.

At that moment, I thought of pushing my child out of my body. Screaming and yet so happy I'd soon be free of her. She slid from me, sweeping out of my body with blood and slick, slipping away from my nest of bones. I knew I'd check out of the hospital in the morning and flee this life and flee her. And there was a very brief moment when I looked at her damp, bloodslicked fuzz of hair, the back of her head, and I nearly let my heart unzip. Instead I shut it down for good until years later, when I saw this baby's skull in *its* nest of bones. There, holding it to my chestbone, my heart snapped open of its own accord, and it is killing me.

When I left that woman and that child, I was different. I went back to the truck, and I stared at Alejandra as if for the first time. As if seeing humanity for the first time. I began to mother her. It's that simple: the sorrow and beauty of it cracked me apart. The whole thing was like a burst of red lightning that streaked through my body and tore my own nest apart. I was surprised at how fragile it was built, how everything was so loosely linked.

*

I climb out of my sleeping bag with throat closing and vomit rising. I'm not built for this. I am built for happy times, for partying and for strong men with sparks in their eyes. I am built for times other than these.

I put on an old red pair of tennis shoes that Libby offered me and pace around the yard, sweating and freezing, wiping snot from my nose, digging my fingers in between the bones of my ribcage. How do stars burn cold? How do I burn so cold? I stumble into Amber's little-girl bike. I walk it down the bumpy dirt driveway and past the cattle-guard and out onto the paved county road, where I start pedaling. My knees go up too far, my gut hurts, my head is pounding. The snot runs faster. The sweat pours. The temperature drops, and I begin to shake.

In the moonlight, I singsong: *Calm, Tess, calm. Try to calm. Stick like a bur to your body.*

The earth smells like rainmelt. Like coldwet dog nose. Like sage and yucca. Like wet cottonwood leaves. I get past the dirt driveway and onto the paved county road and ride and ride and ride. I pedal alongside the moonlit fields of NoWhere, Colorado. A dead skunk in the road, the smell sweeping with me for a good long time. A flattened snake. Cattle that look up to regard me silently in the moonlight. Fields of green winter wheat, just getting tall and growing at this odd time of year. Past dry pastureland, a lone horse standing at the V of a fence. Puddles glisten in the road from time to time, and the bike's tires slosh through. But to the side, where there is earth, the skin of the earth, the water has been absorbed, seeping into the rockbones underneath, the rockbone of the moon above.

It is all one blur, one motion, one dance, all singing. Our one big quest is simply this: Who is going to love me?

Maybe I do love the moon, the rockbones, the spine of the earth.

Perhaps I do love Alejandra and Slade and Libby and Amber.

It's possible I notice small things, such as the way Ed walks like he's hearing some kind of cakewalk music.

The way Slade pulls me into his chest, whispers kind things in my ear.

Maybe I love even Tess and will be sorry to see her go.

A sudden rise of choking fear. I can't breathe. I stop the bike and look around. I'm lost. The landscape is so big. I stand with my legs spread over the bike, steadying myself. Close my eyes. Lean over and throw up the dinner. One spasm, two, three. Gasp for sagesweet, smoky air.

I close my eyes and focus, draw a map of lines in the darkness of my brain. The direction of the mountains, the direction of Lamar, the school, the road to Libby's house, the road to the old house we grew up

in, the road to the place Baxter lived, which is where Kay will be now.
I need a compass. I need my instinct. East-then-south. Heartpounder,
gutwrencher. Breathe, Tess, breathe, don't go flying off into the stars.
      IN THE BEGINNING, Tess was oblivious.
      Tess knew that women gringa drivers were less suspicious.
      Tess was in high demand.
      Tess supposed she knew about how humans get packed
            between hay bales on semi-trucks, frozen in refriger-
            ated trucks, that people die of heat and thirst in
            the desert.

      But she never saw a woman and a baby and a dream
      cut to the bone like that.

      How many men-in-ties
      suddenly realize their culpability?
      Women in dress suits?
      Bankers? Politicians? People in board meetings and
            people in elevators and people screaming at kids?

      How many ways are there to be culpable?
      How many people brought that woman to her knees?
      The details are stuck on Tess's tongue.
      They'll never come out.

Chapter Nine

The bike wheels snap gravel as I turn into the driveway to Baxter's farmhouse. I get off the bike, stagger, catch my balance, look to the stars, stunned by cold, stunned my directions were right, stunned that the house still sits, stunned that it looks like the same old whitebox-farmhouse, stunned by the way it glows in the moonlight, stunned by the light coming from one window, stunned by the familiar cricket-noise and the wisps of cool air coming from the creek.

I walk in the open door, grab a coat hanging on a hook, clasp the puff of down jacket to me. Shiver into it my bonedeep chill. It's only then that I can take in the room. Kay sits in an armchair, lamplit, and I slap a hand over my mouth to trap the noise my surprised breath will make.

Can a person change so much? Her hair is shaved close, has thinned to scalp. A sore underneath her nose, red and puffy, throbs out from her face, and her lips are drawn tight even as she sleeps. Her leg is propped up on a cushion, the sweatpants pulled up, and there is a purple bruise on her ankle surrounded by yellow skin. Three of her toes are missing, the skin pulled tight over the lumps that are left.

Behind her chair is a metal hanger from which dangles a plastic bag full of some clear liquid. To the side is a hospital bed, piled with tubes and boxes.

Tess is glad for this moment,

to see this without having to fix her face.

Tess formed and grew in Kay's body once.

The womb is the opposite of the desert.

Oh, how she used to be! Her hair that brightwhited early, pony-tailed, wisps of it hanging around her face, which made her seagreen eyes flare. Beautiful when riding her horse. Or when dressed up to go out dancing. Or standing in the kitchen, cooking from time to time. But so angry, so frustrated by being alive in the world, so bitter that the world did not conform to her expectations.

When I take my eyes from her missing toes and look back at her face, I see she's opened her eyes. She regards me, hoists an eyebrow. "Don't let the bugs in."

I glance at the bugs buzzing around the light, the big rising moon outside, and I close the screen door and then the wooden door after it. Before I turn back toward her, I breathe in. "OhKay."

She rubs her hands on her face. "It's the middle of the night."

I nod, yes.

"Libby said you were here. It's been ten years, Tess."

I glance over my shoulder, at the door.

"No." Kay lifts a hand weakly from her face into the air, then lets it drop on her lap. "Don't go. Sit down. Tess, you're shivering." She nods to a blanket, which I grab and wrap around the coat. "You look lousy. Pale. Skinny. I see your hair is turning gray too. You saw Amber, I suppose? Your own daughter."

"Oh-by-god." But I keep it at a murmur, beneath my breath, so she can't hear it. I glance around, keep my eyes off her, try to place why this feeling is familiar. Oh, yes—Libby looking at me yesterday—and a strange gurgle of déjà vu rattles over me. This is what it felt like to be Libby, seeing something that hurt the eyes.

Kay shifts in her chair, and the quiet moan from her wet throat is a purr of pain. "What's wrong with you? You dying too? You drunk? Why does it smell like smoke outside?"

I breathe in, sturdy myself. "Wildfire. There's a wildfire in the mountains." My voice stutters from the cold, and I press my lips close.

"Smoke all the way here, huh?"

"Yeah."

"The West is one big firepit now." Her voice is that of someone fading, fading into sleep or death, but she tries to rouse herself. "Amber doesn't smile enough. No one notices that." She leans back, closes her eyes. "I guess neither did you. Smile enough, that is. Neither did any of us." Then she closes her eyes and says, "I'm so tired. Why don't you pour us a whiskey? It's hidden in the stove." Then, "Don't just stand there, giving me your pity. I know how I look. I know what's happening. This is what death looks like. This is what death smells like. Face it." She waves her bony hand toward the kitchen. "I hid it from Libby and Ed. Puritans. I nearly quit for a long while."

I nod in slow motion, turn and walk into the kitchen. Mygod, it has the same old linoleum floor from the '50s, big gray flowers on a cream white background, and that mesmerizes me, the memories of my childhood self, loving those big blooms for their beauty, sitting on those flowers and talking to Baxter. One moment in particular flies into my head. I'm allowed to chalk the flowers, chalk them pink and light orange and green, with big hunks of chalk, and how I chalked my toes, too, chalked Baxter's shoes as he sat reading the paper, how he looked at me and laughed sweetly and said, "It'll wash off, kid. Don't you do this with crayons, only the chalk, and I wouldn't do it around Kay."

I look from the gray blooms to the rest of the room, wide old countertops and old porcelain sink. It is different, though, too, and it takes a moment to register the stacks of white-foam boxes. I peer in. Latex gloves and gauze and alcohol pads and syringes and canisters of hand-san.

"Scrub your hands." Kay is trying to yell it, but her voice is weak and thin. "Especially your cuticles. Use the hand-san. And turn off the faucet with your elbow."

I rinse out two glasses that I find in a dusty cupboard. Stare at the boxes. I can't help the vomit rising up my throat. I swallow it down, but it rises again, and eventually I have to hold my hair back from my face and puke in the sink.

> She's a skeleton, a skeleton.
> Death is probably tickled pink
> by everyone's efforts to avoid him.
> Probably he's a really nice guy.
> Hold it together, Tess, hold it together.

In between heaves, I hear "Cripes, Tess—" and then, "I should have known," and "Clean up your mess."

I rinse out the sink, rinse out my mouth, rinse off my face. I'm not drunk. Just bikepedaling thirsty, soulwrenched. I very much want to be, though. Want to be drunk. I find the whiskey, pour us two glasses, grab a box of crackers, and go back out to the living room. It's the same ragtag-olivegreen carpet that Baxter had when he lived here.

Our fingers touch when I hand her a glass. I raise my arms, let them settle by my sides. Look out the window at the night, at the bugs flying in the beam of the single light on the outside of the shed.

Kay clears her throat and waits until I turn to her. "Let's drink," she says. "Cheers. So, Amber was open to seeing you?"

My stomach churns, not wanting the whiskey as much as the rest of my body does. "Yeah, she was."

"What she needs to do is go ballistic. Cuss you out."

"I suppose."

"As should I. But as you can see, I got enough trouble on my hands. So if you're bringing any trouble yourself, or want any sympathy, you can forget that. And if you're going to act like you have a chip on your shoulder, which is how you've been acting since the day you were born, you can just leave."

I flop into a chair, across from her, and stare. Drink. Regard her.

I pop my neck. "Amber says you stepped on a nail."

"It's true. And then I went fishing. That's what I want my death certificate to say: Nail and fish." Her eyes light up for a flicker of a moment, and she sadly laughs. "Sounds somehow like Jesus, doesn't it?" She sighs and scratches her arm. In the lamplight, I see the flakes of skin rise and then settle. "Getting older is just dealing with new kinds of pain. But yes, I stepped on a nail. Nearly went all the way through my foot. Through the sole of my shoe. Foot swelled up. Libby dragged me to the hospital. Got it cleaned up, got antibiotics. But then it came back. Then I went fishing. A lark—hadn't been for years. Waded in. Because it was hot. Is that such a crime? Well, now that I've had time to reflect on it, perhaps it was. Because you never should forget that the earth can kill you."

"And?" I sip the whiskey, place a cracker on my tongue. Oh, relief. The buzz is good now, a nice head spin, a bodysoftening.

Another sigh. "My foot streaked purple. There's a new strain of staph. There's a bad one called MRSA you get in hospitals. But there's a new one, in Colorado's rivers, called CA-MRSA. Or something like that." She stares off into space, breathes in. "I've been in many hospitals, for many days. I guess some people should just die. The world is too crowded." She closes her eyes out of pain. A tightness between the eyebrows, a sorrow seeping through eyelids. "But it's harder than you think. You're lucky I'm sick. Otherwise, I might not be so forgiving. You sure are one shithead for leaving like that. All this time, with no way to contact you. I couldn't even tell you about Baxter's funeral. He loved you so much, you know. And he never got to tell you goodbye." She opens her eyes briefly.

I know I should voice words, find my vocalchord voice. "Where's he buried?"

"Ashes scattered across this place. Where the pretty rock outcrop is. That's where I want to be scattered too." She scratches her thigh, looks at her foot. "Ugly, isn't it? He was always telling me that he asked his guardian angel to leave him and go follow you. 'That Tess,' he'd say, 'She's giving our guardian angels gray hairs, and I can hear them bitching about it now.'"

That makes me smile. "Yeah, that sounds like him." Then, after a pause, "You can have them back, now, the guardian angels. Seems like you need them more."

She holds an ice chunk in her cheek. "I used to not worry about death. But here I am. At the door. And it's not easy. Tess, if the alcohol-and-pain-pill mix gets me, well, know it was my choice. It's a nice, neat, no-questions-asked-after way. You know? But still. I guess I should have prepared more."

Pause, pause. Can't argue that. Finally, "It's your life. As you used to tell me."

"It was," she says quietly. "I suppose I wasted it. I suppose I always felt like I'd gotten the shaft or deserved better. Nothing ever went my way. Never got much of a break. Lord knows I tried. I suppose you know what I mean."

The nonsurprise of her saying such a thing sends me up and to the window staring at the moon, and it reminds me of my theory formed on the bus here, about cavernous apologies and thank yous meaning diddlyshit unless you voice them to the appropriate person. Kay never did, and she never will. Perhaps Kay knows what I'm thinking, because just to drive the point home, she adds, "You were always a little shit," which once-upon-a-time would have sent me storming out, but now I stand firm and keep my eyes trained on the moon.

> The joys and love Tess expected
> from life
> were arid nothings.
> The lifejoy turned out to be badly placed.

> But it was Tess's job to change her expectations,
> and she didn't.

*

"Tell me one thing about your life." Kay says this after a few hours of us both drifting in and out of sleep. "So I can try to understand you. Libby will be here sooner or later. Before she gets here, just tell me one true thing. The kind of thing you wouldn't want her to hear."

I sip the whiskey. The blurbuzz of the alcohol has been established, and it must be for her, too, otherwise she wouldn't ask something so real. The alcohol in my blood helps with my goal of giving her the respect of looking at her, though my eyes keep wanting to dart away.

I open my mouth. I want to form the words. I want to ask her: Did you ever feel any motherlove?

Kay looks at me, sharply. "Say something, Tess. Something real."

But I shake my head, no. She closes her eyes and does not open them.

*

The room has settled into the sounds of predawn. Crickets, birds, an awakening of the earth itself. Kay winces, shifts. She pokes her finger into her leg. "It used to be hot all the way up to the knee. The heat is moving down. Got any open wounds? Keep 'em covered, if you do. This is contagious." Much later, she rouses herself and says, "Every Saturday, Libby scrapes off my skin. My skin tries to cover the wound, and she scrapes it right off. Because the wound needs to heal from the bottom up. Having skin cover it will just keep the infection buried in the body. She's still hoping I'll live."

I clear my throat. "There was a young girl I helped. That I loved once. Named Alejandra. I loved her whistles," I say. "I loved her language. She invented words, just like I did as a kid. She'd say the funniest things—'Come on, guys, show some leaderism!'—when she wanted the group to perk up. When you did something dumb, she would say, *'Estupiota!'* When she wanted the radio turned up, she would say, 'Loud it up!' She would say 'limitated' when she meant limited. When she wanted to eat something, she would say, 'Where are some gobbles?' As in, where are some snacks I can gobble?"

"That's funny. Like you used to be. I don't know what happened."

I look at her, cold. *You did,* I almost say. *You happened.*

But Libby's quiet footfall makes us turn. She's on her way to work, in her nurse outfit, walking in the door quietly. Without stopping, she gives us a chirpy "Good morning" and me a "You rode Amber's bike over?" and gives me a look that means *It's good you came here* and *I know about the fire.* Then she moves to the kitchen, returns with a plastic bag. "I'm going to flush out the tubing with saline and hook up a new bag," she says. "I'll teach you later, if you want to learn."

Kay murmurs, "I know you wish I'd just die."

Libby's hands move over Kay, one fluid motion. She's graceful, even in her hurry. "Bodies can and do heal."

"Don't bullshit a bullshitter. Well, *I* want me to die." Kay closes her eyes. "I'm so unhappy. I'm so uncomfortable." Then she glances at me. "So how do you feel about your runaway sister coming back? What do you think she wants from us?"

Libby keeps working with the clear plastic bag she's hanging. She looks beautiful in this morning light—someone who is doing something, who has a purpose, who has a reason. Her hair is in a raggedy ponytail, and she's still got on her cheapbrand tennis shoes, but somehow in the nurse outfit, and when she moves so efficiently, she glows.

She glances at me. "Tess, the drip is set for every two seconds. Kay always tries to speed it up, but don't let her touch anything. It needs to drop at two seconds." She waits until I nod, then turns to wrap the bandage around Kay's wound with a little flair. She tucks the edge under in one swift movement.

"It's too damn slow." Kay closes her eyes. Her words are blurry, marred with the little bit of alcohol she had, the mix with pain meds. "It's so painful. What kind of god would make us hurt so much?"

"Exactly," I murmur.

"This is the PICC line." Libby holds up the plastic tubing. "It can-*not* get infected. It's an opening right into Kay's core. And if it gets infected, Kay gets sepsis, and she dies. Okay? Kay, you cannot open the drop to be too fast."

Kay looks at her. "Libby, ask us if we've been drinking." Then, "We sipped whiskey all night! I fess up. I'm drunk from exhaustion, and drunk from whiskey, and drunk from this dying business."

Libby looks above Kay, as if examining the walls for patience and love. "I'm going to work," she says. "Tess, there are bedrooms upstairs. Sheets might be dusty, but they're clean enough. We'll see you tonight? Perhaps we could bring over some food and all eat here. Together."

"No!" Kay's voice startles us both. She moves herself in her chair, grunting. "Tess, I think you owe your sister an apology. I want to hear it."

I look at her. Bite my tongue. I look up at Libby, tilt my head. "She'll never change, will she? But you did. And that's what I came for. To see it. Also, to come home and say something real. We used to care for each other, didn't we, Libby? When we were kids? Because each other is all we had? You were a good sister. You protected me. And Kay, you were a lousy mother, and I turned into a thickskinned fuck." I look at the ceiling. "And Libby kept taking care of me, because you didn't. Then she took care of my kid. And the kid turned out great. I look like shit, and Kay looks like shit, and Libby looks like a happy woman stuck with a bunch of responsibility but with a real genuine life. Ed is good, and Amber is good. Thank god for that. I thank you, Libby, for your courage. That's the core of what I want to say."

Libby keeps her eyes on the wall behind me, turns, and leaves. Kay mumbles some quick farewell, and Libby lets the screen door shut gently. I let out a whistle that will carry to her as she walks away. *I love you*, it means, although she doesn't know that. I see her pause, hear it, and keep going, toward her truck and toward the mountains, which are blurred with haze from fire.

PART III

Fire

Chapter Ten

What would be the relief in redemption if it were a simple *sorry, forgive me*? Grace is not achieved so easily. Redemption is to purchase back something previously sold, the recovery of something pawned or mortgaged, the effort it takes to make things right. Bless me, self, for trying to reacquire some of what I sold somewhere along the line.

*

I wait for Slade's whistle to strike my eardrums. I listen while I do Kay's dishes, laundry, bring her tea, sweep the gray blooms. My ears ache with the seeking, with standing to attention, like an alert deer in a road, holding her position, large ears tipped, knowing there's danger coming, exhausted by the stillness required to catch the very first moment of sound, the one that will tell her which way to go.

Enough time has now passed, hasn't it? His realization I was gone, him finding the empty van in Alamosa, his figuring out where I'd be. Wouldn't something guide him here? The fire in his loins? The fire in his heart? The fire in the mountains? But no: I had spoken my goodbyes. Told him we were over. That I was doing this last run and then was gone. This last kiss and then was gone. I had made my list of people to say goodbye to and in which order—Slade, Libby, Amber— and he was the first to get the news.

I listen but hear only Kay's soft moans. She drifts in and out. Speaks and stares off into silence. Says a few words, kind and unkind. Directs me to do this, to do that. My feet pad across old carpeting, across linoleum, across wood floors, and I listen. I hear the wind, the flies buzzing, a siren far away on the highway. I hear the radio speaking of the fire, of the raging, uncontainable fire, the new lightning-started fires, how the people and animals of Colorado are fleeing down, away, trucks and trailers, helicopters and buses, Greyhound and schoolbus alike, donated, offered, given. Ranchers' phone numbers spray-painted on horses and cattle, fences cut so those animals can make their way down, there no longer being time to round them up and haul them out. Everything, everyone, moving away from the crackling storming whooshing, from the choking air, from the bloom of red.

He's not coming. You need to say your goodbyes. Hold yourself together. Don't fragment. I say it again and again to myself as I watch my hands move in their chores, as I watch my feet cross the floors.

Kay and I watch one another, even when our eyes are not meeting. One full day with one another, which is not something I ever recall happening. She sees what she needs to see, perhaps: her daughter, too skinny and pale, able to move around a kitchen, able to sit and flip through a magazine, able to make light conversation. She does not ask about where I've been or where I'm going. She does not tell me where she's been or where she's going, in regard to her heart. Has it changed at all? I see what I need to see: a woman who is diminished, in pain, weakened. I cannot see inside her. I cannot know if, as I used to believe, she is still stuck in her belief that she was alone on the planet, and that she particularly got the shaft. If her *me* was ever replaced by *other*. If *self* was replaced by love or kindness or compassion. If, like me, she could see the lack and tried to fill it. If ever she has larger or grander ideas about others—her daughters, for example, and how they might be experiencing the world.

She seems much the same but drugged, still like a bulldog, so ready to attack the world, so much energy put into crashing through life, and her old words roil around in my mind: *I'm paying our bills, feeding you snotty kids, working my ass off, and for what? What joy do I get out of this?*

I watch her fiddle with her iPod, sigh, bored. She doesn't enjoy the book she's listening to. Doesn't like NPR. Doesn't like music. Her deathmap is the opposite of mine. She is resigning herself into it, slowly, like irrigation water seeping across a field. Me, I'll be a sudden burst of fire.

"Forgive her," Baxter said to me once, when I was a teenager. "She's so tired that she doesn't have any energy for kindness, and kindness is actually a lot of work." He was sweeping up our house, having just come from cleaning his, and he said, "Kindness actually takes an enormous amount of energy, Tess, but it's always worth it. It's like an elemental energy. Like wind, like fire, like water. And you know why we seek it? The same way we seek water and air? Because we get our butts kicked by life, and someone helps us out. And we realize we need people, and therefore they need us. Kindness is one of the basic elements. And we very quickly realize that it makes no sense to be selfish. No sense at all. It's useless to be selfish. So we work hard to mitigate the ass-kicking-ness of life for other people. That's why I'm here sweeping. You sweep things up too."

I listen to the birdsong, to the flies buzzing, and I think, *Baxter, that coupla lines I will never forget.* I didn't live them, but I heard them.

Slade was my one heartsweeper. He knew the dusty corners.

But there's no whistle, just one full day of Kay. One full day of letting Amber go to school, Libby and Ed attend to their life, of brief phone calls to confirm and chat through all this. One day of knowing the mountains burn. One full day of holding pattern. Trying to notice it all. Trying to be kind. Trying to outgrow my mother and her hold on my heart.

At dusk I stop cleaning and stand at the doorway to watch the sky turn. In front of me is the driveway, the circle of outbuildings. Beyond that is the alfalfa field. To the right is the old corral where we used to run cattle through, me always a reluctant participant, and to the left is a longstretch of pasture of grasses and occasional yucca and brittlebush. All of it shifts color as the sky turns. Funny, this transformation of late. My heart turning in the same slow way. All this time, so tough. Five years since the skeleton. Five years of fading in and out of my body. *I can't make it much longer. I just don't want to go on much longer. I'll go out with a bang.* Jutting out my chin. Giving the world a *fuck you* look. Like my mother. And then two weeks ago sitting in the dentist office, a toothache searing my sanity away, and I pick up a little book of wisdoms that he had sitting in his waiting room, and I read, *Use death as your advisor, and you'll start making better decisions about your life,* and I have the simple clear thought: I want to leave Amber some real money, I want to go see her, I want to tell Libby goodbye, I want to tie up loose ends, sweep up the clutter. I want to go home. I want to go home before I decide what to do next, being pretty sure what my next step will be, but first I want to go home. I can't use the old Colt .38—I told Libby I wouldn't ever use that on myself—but I'll find another way. I know plenty of ways.

But now these tears, these pangs of emotion in my heart. A full decade without them, and now they keep showing up, uninvited. I touch the tender bump on my forehead, run my fingers across my grated-up cheek: evidence of when I could only hurt on the outside.

Now that I'm nearing the end, though, I feel hurt crashing around the inside and close my eyes to concentrate. Right then, the piercing note of a whistle cascades through the air.

*

Heartfade.

Heartjump.

I hear the air escape my body. An ohthankgodyes. I hear the follow-up string of notes. I take a step from the house. The sound comes from across the alfalfa field, over by the old house of childhood, a mile away at the small dark square I still barely see in the fading light.

Libby, I scribble on a piece of paper, *Out for a long walk because it was a long day. Plus I want to see this landscape and all the old haunts again. See you all tomorrow, dearheart?*

My dearheart sister, which is what I've been calling her since I was a child, probably as soon as she taught me such words. She won't be surprised, my long nightwalks always being the sign of coping with the day. I pin the paper to the coffeetable with a cup and grab a coat and shove the nearly empty bottle of whiskey deep into the pocket. On my way out, I pull on a hat, gloves. I throw a last glance at Kay, who is sleeping in the same chair she has been in most of the day besides short trips to the bathroom or kitchen. In her sleep, she looks open, human.

I slip out the screen door and take in the night. I whistle, listen. Walk, trip, walk again. Zigzag my way around Kay's house, outbuildings, toward the alfalfa, toward the old house. I hug the jacket tighter around me. It's true, what Slade taught me. The sound of the human voice can be hard to pinpoint, and land absorbs and changes and shifts around the sound waves, but a whistle travels straight.

Bless Slade for being smart, bless him for being kind. Smart and kind enough to read my most obvious thoughts: *Don't bring the danger to where my kid and sister are; meet me at the old place.* A small sweet coincidence that he knows where that is at all. We had been on a drive together, and we'd just left the *pollos* in Lamar. "Let's stop and see your family, we're right here anyway," he'd said. *No thanks, mister.* "Well, let's at least drive by your old place. Show me where you grew up?" *Nope.* He pulled over, regarded me calmly. Dark eyes raised. "I won't move this car, honeyheart, until you tell me where your homeplace is. You need to learn to share yourself." I was startled by that, enough to tell him the location, and we drove by, slowly, and he saw the old house of my childhood, saw that it was still junked up, although Libby, who was living there at the time, had painted the house purple, and had gotten a swing set too. Slade had said, "Really? Tess? No joke? You don't want to see them? They're right there," and I said, *Drive on, sir, get me out of this place,* and he gave me a sad look and did what he was told.

Even if he didn't remember the road, he could put the puzzle pieces together. How it was across the alfalfa field from Baxter's place, how he might have watched it, noticed it was abandoned now. How perhaps he might have been smart enough to locate Kay's address. How he would have driven by Libby and Ed's home and known not to stop. We could often read each other this way. He's good at that sort of thing. *A natural private detective,* he used to say; it was a point of pride, it was good business. *We are good together, kid.*

I whistle back, and he whistlereplies, until I've walked nearly a mile and see a small fire in a gully outside of the old house, at the very spot where Libby and I used to play, carving out caves in the dirt and playing house. Little Mesa Verde homes and peoples. I haven't seen that old childhood house for ten years now, besides that drive-by with Slade, and it startles me, the shadowy outline of it in the moonlight, the sameness of it, the memories.

I stop. Look all around me. Behind me, the moon is higher, no longer red. Slade sits in front of the fire in a lawn chair, a cooler to his left, and his black pickup truck is backed up into a little grove of trees nearby, concealed. He has the topper on it for sleeping. His headlamp is directed down at his feet. He's waiting for me, perhaps even knowing that I'm looking at him. He's in a peagreen wool coat and has a blanket wrapped around him, a bottle of beer in one hand, a joint in the other. Now he looks up, out into the darkness, waiting for me or my next whistle or acknowledging my presence. But I'm not yet ready to move. If I stare long enough in the silence, I can see past all those big brushstrokes of an image. I can see the particulars. I can see his face in the fireflashes. There is a real man, a strong and good man, a man who has seen realshit and who can still be tender. He wipes his nose, runs his hand over his cheek, down his sideburns that I know will be shaved at an angle. I think of the times I have held his head, have run my fingers through his air, against his soft-prickly jaw, his chin and upper lip emblazoned with a few days of scruffle, which makes my chin and nose red after kissing, and then the dark hair starting at his neck and blooming all over his chest. Of course, this is all hidden. Hat and coat and blanket. But underneath all that is his naked body, strong and broad shouldered.

The one thing I can't see is the look in his eyes. He taught me that: If you can catch a person's eyes before they register your presence, before they can firm up, you'll see their true emotion, what they really think of you. But you have to get them in that split second.

I almost step into view but pause. Consider. Always, always assess the situation before walking in. Never assume a thing. I look and listen for evidence of others. Mark the distance between human and vehicle. Decide where the keys are likely to be. Decide where the guns are likely to be. Decide where I'd run if I had to, decide how I'd attack if I had to.

But Slade is alone, and so I step forward. As soon as I step into the light, he stands up and comes toward me, arms raised in a hug.

"You had the GPS wrong." His voice is calm, measured, as it always is. Always with confidence, always within his own custody.

I breathe out a long sigh. "Please tell me that's not true." I press myself into his chest.

He holds me, rocks me back and forth. Then he opens up another camping chair that he has sitting out and gestures to sit, but before I can, he bearhugs me again, rocks me again. "Oh, Tess," he says into the top of my hair. "Oh, Tess, it's really bad."

I look up into his face, and he guides me to the chair, gently forces me to sit. Sits in his, leans over, takes my hand. "I honestly don't know, Tess. I don't know what happened. I don't know where it went wrong." His voice is low and steady. "If I transposed a number, or if you did, or if Lobo did. It was either you, me, or Lobo. Or the *pollos* wandered off, I guess. I don't know. They got hungry. They were desperate." His eyes seem to focus only on my hand. "They were one valley to the west. They lit a signal fire to be found." He squeezes my fingers, swings my arm, and we look like two schoolkids sitting and holding hands and swinging arms, a sad and strange swing.

I feel as calm and worn-out as these windblown rocks around us. "I heard on the radio. But how do the police know that? Did they survive?"

He scratches his jaw. "They're missing."

"But that means they're dead—"

"No, it means they're missing."

"But how did someone know?"

He shrugs and for a long time sits in silence. Then he gestures to his lap. It's his invitation, firm and yet tender, and so I respond, put my butt in his lap, fold my legs over the armrest of his chair. He holds my body, so small against his. "They got a call. A woman. Saying that she admitted they had come over the border, that they were a group of seven, that they were starving, that they'd started a signal fire so that they could be found, that they were sorry, to please come help."

"And then?"

"Well, I guess the law headed up there and found a fire raging."

I press my cheek into his chest, and his fingers find the scratch on my other one.

"Slade, I'm so sorry. I was a little drunk the first coupla hours, I admit. But I felt alert. I had that sheet of paper from the little notebook. I was there, Slade, I was there." Then, "How angry are you?"

"I'm not angry." He says it quietly, his finger now tracing the edge of the scratch, my own finger tracing the edge of his goatee. "But, Tess—"

"Oh, Slade. I was *there*. I'd been at that spot before. Right next to an old adobe house in ruins, right where the airplanes do the dope drops. Right on Devil's Road, *Camino del Diablo*. Isn't that where I was supposed to be? I waited. I waited and I waited. For three days. Why didn't you come up? Were you still on that other run?" I had left him his stuff—his .40-caliber Glock, night-vision goggles, bulletproof vest, GPS—at his trailer outside of Alamosa. The immigrants had never shown up, and so I'd taken everything back, dumped it on his living room floor, so that he could never accuse me of taking anything. I could tell he hadn't been home in a while, I knew he was on a run of his own, and besides, I had told him that this would be my last, and that we were over, and that I never wanted to see him again. Which is something I'd told him a coupla times over the years, but this time I knew I was on my lastchance trip home, so perhaps I sounded firmer and surer. Then I'd hitchhiked to the bus station and slept with the first guy I met so I could steal his wallet and use that money for a ticket home. While on the bus, well, that's when I told myself: three days of sweeping up. And if there is no home to go to, then play your last card.

He's running a finger along the nape of my neck. "Yes, I was gone on my own run. I didn't understand why you suddenly up and left. Plus, I had work to do. I didn't know you needed help. I showed up at the trailer, and there was all my stuff. I couldn't figure out why. You should have been in Denver by then, dropping them off. I was worried that they would have made you carry the *coca*, which is something I told you never to do. The other guy was supposed to come get that."

"Well, *no* one came, Slade. Not one of Lobo's men. No *pollos*. No one at all. I was just so alone . . . it was so quiet . . . and I walked and hummed and waited and slept in the van . . . and my tooth felt like a motherfucker . . . and I just kept getting more and more . . ."

"Fragmented?"

"Yeah." Then, "I couldn't even call to tell you that they didn't show."

"I know, sweetheart. Listen, Tess. I gotta tell you something." He pushes me away from him so that I have to look him in the eye. "That's why I came all the way out here. Even if you don't want to see me again, even if you said your goodbye. I gotta tell you something, and then I gotta disappear. As you should too. Although—" and here, he laughs a sad laugh, "I'm pretty sure it's going to break you for good." He stares into the fire. "Too painful. Too painful even for me."

I look up at him and snort. What possibly could be worse now? Nothing. No-thing.

He pulls the sleeping bag over us, then a green wool army blanket that's been sitting out. "First, of course, we've got law all over the fucking place. I don't know about Lobo. He's a wildcard. Those *pollos* were carrying a lot of product. I'm trying to piece it together. There they are, bunch of drugs with them, and no one picks them up. They're at the wrong location or whatever. So they start to get serious hungry and thirsty and so they start a signal fire." There's something mesmerizing about his voice. "You wanna drink, baby?"

"What's this thing you need to tell me?"

He hands me a beer, but I drink from the whiskey bottle instead. "I'm surprised you'd come here. I thought you were never going to see any of them again," he says. "Although, no. That's not true. I knew to

come here, didn't I? As a last resort, everyone heads home. Oh, baby.
We fucked up. Or no, maybe it's just that it got fucked up." He pokes
right below his chest, at his sternum, where he thinks his intuition lies.
His best brain, he calls it. His true sense. "I knew to come here. Didn't
know what the fuck to do, actually. But I had to get out of there, and I
had nowhere to go, and my instinct, man, it just drove me here. To this
little eastern Colorado town. Same as your instinct."

"Tell me, Slade."

"No, wait. First. Tell me. What's going on here, at your home?"

I drink and close my eyes so I can appreciate the moment when
my cells relax. There's nothing he can tell me that will kill me any
faster. There's nothing he can say, and so I oblige. "Kay's dying.
Libby and Ed welcomed me, reluctantly. Amber is beautiful. It's
good you came here, and not by Ed and Libby's. Thank you. They
walk around too much. The very least I could do is protect them from
all this. Kay, on the other hand, is not going to be snooping around.
You're safe here."

He takes my hand and holds it, cupped, in his two. "Tess, everyone needs to see their mama once. Instinct. This is gonna be hard." He
pauses, moves his jaw in a circle, looks above my head, back at me. "It
wasn't just any group of *pollos*, Tess."

"What?"

He looks at me with a sick feeling on his face, his eyes lowered. "It
was a surprise for you, baby. I had it all planned. Then you broke up
with me."

I blink at him. "I don't know what you're talking about—"

"Your girl. And her mama. Plus their cousins and brothers—"

I blink again, first at him, and then at the stars.

"Listen. This was my surprise for you. My gift. I knew you liked
them. Loved Alejandra, in fact. They had contacted Lobo to get them
across. I even paid half their way. You were going to go up there, and

see them, and transport them one last time. It was supposed to be beautiful." He laughs a sad, bitter moan. "A *coyote*'s version of a gift, I guess. A couple of people you actually want to see."

"You liar. They're in Mexico."

"No, they're not. They've been trying to get across for months. I was helping them . . . find the right people . . . well, you know. I didn't want any chance of rape, which is pretty hard to—well, you know. It took all this extra effort." He holds my hand tight, tighter still when I try to jerk away. "I got a letter at the trailer. Addressed to you, but I opened it because that was during the time you were gone, out wandering. They wanted to come back to the States. Mother and daughter. Start a life here. So I thought I'd surprise you. I contacted Lobo, and all the *coca y mota* was set up, and cousins to carry it, to help pay the way."

"You're lying."

"I'm not."

"It wasn't them in the mountains."

"They're probably . . . Oh, sweetheart—" He stops and starts again. "Along with a lot of product. Not that that matters. Except it does, because that's what Lobo is gonna come looking for. That was a lotta money, babe. A lot. And so that's the other thing I came to tell you. You gotta go. We both gotta disappear."

I am up and hitting him on the head and face and chest.

Slade tries to pull me to him, tries to gather in my fury, holds me to the point of pain until I still. "Oh, babe. It was supposed to be a good surprise."

I elbow him in the ribs, and his gasp sends me into a crawling lurch away from him, away from the fire. I stumble to the truck, heave myself through the little door into the back, scramble around. *Where is it, where is it?* My old Colt .38 that Libby gave me to protect myself? My alltime favorite. Gunmetal blue. I named it *Salvador*, Ed's name.

Slade is at the back of the truck, peering in. "It's not loaded. Of course it's not loaded."

My hands are flying around in the lockbox. My fingers close around the little rectangle, and at that moment, Slade reaches in the back of the truck, grabs my ankle, and pulls me out, hard. He holds me to him. "I'm sorry." He says it over and over. "I'm sorry, Tess, I'm sorry." Later, he says, "It's possible they're alive. Maybe they ran." And later, when my knees give out, he catches my weight. He holds me like a baby, stumbling for a moment, and then pushes my limp body against the back of the truck as he struggles to lift me in. He puts a pillow under my head, a sleeping bag over me. Puts the gun back in the lockbox along with everything I tore out of it. He is meticulous, careful, and I watch him wrap the gun and ammo in a soft cloth, put it at the bottom, the flares and firstaid and nightgoggles and headlamps carefully above it. Finally he lies next to me, wraps his arms around me. "I'm sorry. I love you, Tess. Actually. I know you don't believe it, but I do." Later, he says, "I'm sorry." Over and over. He keeps talking, and the planet spins. The universe expands. My heart beats. I snapped a wishbone without a wish.

*

I unzip my pants, push them down, and Slade holds me closer and says, "Go to sleep, Tess, you're drunk." I touch him through his jeans and murmur. "One more time before I die," I say, and he says, "Shhhh, baby. Stop that. You're not gonna die. Is that why you left me? To say goodbye? Well, I'm not going to let you do it." He holds me so tight in his arms that I have to go limp. "You have no choice in the matter," I say. "You know it, and I do too."

When I wake, I open my eyes to find him above me, inside me. His hips are bolted into mine, his deepfuck, when he pushes in and circles, not the backandforth of sex, but the quieter circling. I close my eyes and let my body take over, which is what he wants, which is what his body is doing, circling, our bones pressed so tight that we are nearly just that, bones touching. It's the bones touching that brings my body back into itself, and this is why people have sex—it's not for the orgasm, it's to get this close to redemption. I feel him inside me, the pain it causes, I feel the inflamed tissues of my infection, I feel the inflamed tissue of him, I think of how the blood from my neverending period will be darkrust, like beetle-killed pine trees, now brown and eating up the mountains, and the only time I didn't have a period was when I was carrying Amber, nine months of no blood. Nine months of life, and now it's the end of my blood, it's the full moon, and it's time to go. One last glance at Amber, one note to explain, a last apology, a last request for forgiveness.

Time rolls in on itself, and Slade rolls to the side and tries to hold me, but I turn away, and from the little window of the topper, I can see the nighttime sky.

"Tess," he says, pulling me back toward him. He traces my ear, then taps me on the head. "Mexico. Listen, I've thought this through—"

"No, Slade."

He strokes my hair. "We can survive this. We can change our game plan. We can't start up again here. We can't stay on the run. We get to Mexico. Lord knows I'm set up there. I've got some savings. I've got connections. We live in a small town, in the mountains. We got the blood of people on our hands."

"Slade, no."

"Listen, Tess. You should stay here for a bit. See your daughter and mother and sister and all that. Make your peace. Make amends. Offer them something. I get that. But then, Tess, we leave. Maybe Lobo is gonna let this drop. We don't have the pot or coke, we don't have the money, we don't have the people, we don't have nothing.

So I am guessing he'll leave us alone. But on the other hand, that guy is a maniac."

I roll deeper into the sleeping bag, so that I'm buried down deep, but I can't stop the trembling.

"Maybe he'll let it drop. But you can't stay here. What if he thinks you started the fire? *You* have the drugs? *You* have the *pollos*?"

"It's funny," I hear myself murmur. "You ever think of all the people we crossed? How they must have spent their last days with their family, then saying goodbye, maybe for the last time? They were leaving home to find a new one. They wanted to find a new place to belong. But it's harder to find than they think."

Alejandra. Lupe. Impossible that such beautiful people are dead. "Oh, those poor people, Slade. Poor Alejandra . . ."

(Find a friend, kill it. Grow a friendship, it dies.)

(Seek love, it gets twisted down into earth.)

He pulls me to him, rocks me back and forth in his arms, rests his hand on my hip. "Baby, there's nothing you can do. Going to jail sure as fuck isn't going to help them. It just . . . happened." He holds me even tighter, then puts his nose into my hair. "We both feel like shit right now. We get to Mexico, we adopt some kids. To make up for it. Maybe not adopt them in the formal sense, but you know, take them under our wing. To make up for it." Later, "I'm not a bad man, Tess. We just got messed up in the wrong life."

But the dark details have already bloomed. Humans cowering as the fire sweeps toward them, the heat, the smell, the fear. The screams. But not just any people. Alejandra. The kid who once sat next to me, all skinny with big knees, crooked eyeteeth, yammering away. Skinny legs, bony knees.

The tremors passing through me are earthquakes, the nerves lightning. Slade puts his hand on my shoulder blade and shakes my body, hard. "Don't do it, Tess. Don't do what you're doing. Every time those images come into your mind, picture the face of a kid that you're going to help. Train your brain to go there. Stay calm and go slow." Then, "Say goodbye to your family, Tess. Do it right. Do it well. You were right to come here. Now, you can leave. You can really be free."

The earthquakes and thunder and lightning speak for me: Yes, I know it.

The wind has dropped. The wind has shhhhhsed, the airtemperature is dropping. The smell of soil and of wheat nearby. The Milky Way, the Pleiades. He turns me toward him, hard. "Promise me. Swear to me. Don't do anything for the next few days. See your daughter, your sister, and just pretend the rest of this hasn't happened. And then we'll figure it out."

I nod, but he squeezes, and so I offer him a manysplendored lie. Yes.

Later, much later, when I hear his first snores, I slide out of Slade's arms and the sleeping bag—*oh it's cold, so cold*—and it takes a sheer force of will to climb out of the back of the truck and to put my clothes on and move. One last look: his eyelashes, his scruffly cheeks, his soul.

Chapter Eleven

The stars with their tiny teeth are biting the sky, shining as bright as they can when I make it back to the farmhouse. When I find the keys in the ignition of Kay's truck, a melancholy laugh flutters out of me: Kay's theory on life being that you shouldn't own anything worth stealing, and you never put shit anywhere else than where you use it. The little details of knowing a person.

The door at Libby and Ed's home is unlocked per the same theory. I close it quietly. Ringo darts out at me, but I'm able to say, *Hey now, hey*, before he gets his bark off, and he rings my legs, tail wagging. I orient myself in the house and tiptoe down the hall to Amber's room. Ringo follows me, lifting his head into my hand, jabbing his nose into my crotch to smell.

Amber. It's a cliché thing to do. So be it. I want to see this kid sleep, in the inout of breath, eyes closed, tender.

I move quietly in. She's sprawled on her stomach with a quiet breath coming from her, one arm flung up above her head, hair spread out across her pillow. I want to see what I can feel, to see this child of mine alive and well. Her hand moves a bit, she rolls to the side, makes a noise with her lips, sinks deep again. Her lips are slightly parted. Air. Fire. Wind. Water.

The sky behind her is starting to turn from black to a strange gray. "Back then, I didn't think you'd be enough to fill my heart. Now you would be, I think, but it's too late." I whisper this to Amber in a voice so quiet that not even I can hear. "You are beautiful, though. I'm so sorry I've disappointed you. That's a secret I hadn't told you. There is such a thing as life not worthy to be lived." I reach out, touch her hair like a mother might, let my hand rest there and close my eyes and beg myself to remember this moment at my last. I watch her breathe. In, out. Her hair is a dark cascade on white sheet. In, out.

*

I sit on the couch and pull the cushions over me—so *soft*—and I stare out the window, at the moon thus framed. Ringo flops on the floor, graceless. I feel the pull and sway and dance of it all. Emotion comes and goes like the moon, like the immigrants crossing the border, like the *coyotes* that transport them, like the rotation of the earth itself.

Ringo looks up at me, thumps his tail, watches me as I reach over to find a pen, a slip of Amber's notebook paper.

*

The rosy-fingered dawn. Amber has the book sitting out on the kitchen table, the same Lattimore translation I borrowed off of Libby with some of my handwriting on the inside. Nothing changes that much, not from Greeks to now, not from my childhood to Amber's.

I look out the window. It is, in fact, a rosy-fingered dawn, the curve of earth lighting under a pink glow. I regard the kitchen table, put a Saltine cracker in my mouth, make coffee, take a handful of aspirin, rummage through the fridge. Just this one last day of effort.

Ed wanders down the stairs first, frowsyheaded and handsome from sleep. I have to look away from his tender openness. Libby comes right after, equally as foggy. Ringo stands up from where he's been lying at my feet to greet them. Gives them a hello nudge in the crotch.

"Okay," I hear myself saying. "Fried potatoes. Omelets."

Libby looks at me suspiciously, shoots Ed a look that says something. "Morning," she says. "I thought you were at Kay's."

"Couldn't sleep. Plus, you know, I thought you should eat before you went to work."

"I took off work today."

"To see me?"

She pauses, looks down to pull up her pajama bottoms. "Yes."

Ed pulls on his shoes but looks up from his hunched-over position. "Any word on the fire?"

"It's growing. It's just . . . never going to stop."

"It'll stop." But he looks miserable, and then, without a word, goes outside.

Libby watches him go. "He'll do chores first." Then, as she pours herself coffee, she says, "So, hey, about a month ago, Kay and I went through all her old stuff, to sort it, you know. Pare down. She'd been bugging me for months. I've got two plastic containers. Of yours."

"There's nothing I care about, Libby."

She walks up and tousles my hair. "You look cute this way, with short hair. Some of that old stuff is funny to see again. Old school projects. Artwork. Clay pots and bad clunky things that say 'I love mom' and stuff." She sits down at the table and sips her coffee. "Tess, I think you should see a doctor while you're in town. You're so pale, so thin . . . Just run some blood tests, get a checkup. I'll pay for it."

I give her some line about how as soon as I go to a doctor, it puts all kind of shit into motion, names and social security number, and I've never paid taxes, and I want to be disappeared, so give me a day, and I'll be better. When she objects, I finally agree. It doesn't matter. There will be no test. To distract her, I ask, "Hey, Libby? Are you happy?"

She looks over to see what I'm cooking to hide her surprise. "I'm glad I've taken Amber. If that's what you're asking. Is that what you're really asking? It's been tough, especially those baby years—I didn't particularly like those—but now it's just fun. Actually *fun*. It's fun to hang around a person who is one of the most intelligent, curious, wonderful humans on earth. Plus, it's fun to do everything the exact opposite of Kay. To realize that you can change the pattern."

"So, all in all, it hasn't been a mistake? Wish we'd given her to some other family?"

"No, I've never been sad. Even when it was tough."

"So it's enough? To . . . I don't know, fill you up? Do you know what I mean?"

She looks at me, straight on. "Of course I do. You're not the only one who feels empty, you know. Sometimes I get lonely. Sometimes it still feels like something is missing. The Buddhists say life is suffering. But that's a bad translation. They mean *unsettled*. To want more. To be seeking. For a while, I thought it might be a kid of my own. To carry a baby and then hold it. But I couldn't. We tried to have a baby, and we couldn't. So, see, Amber was a real gift."

My eyebrows move up on their own, my hand reaches out to grab *The Odyssey* to my heart. "Oh, wow. I didn't know."

"How could you? You've been gone ten years with no way to stay in touch. And just so you know, I quit asking for a well-being check from the police. I was afraid it would just get you in trouble. I knew by instinct you were fine and wanted to be left alone."

The potatoes are thinly sliced, burbling around in hot oil. I stab my fork into one, bring it out onto a paper towel, salt it. My stomach feels unsure of food. I tap my chest, hard. "There's a monster that lives there. It feels like there's actually something inside. Anxiety, I suppose. It used to just be in the mornings. Now it's all day."

She looks at me, blinks her doebrown eyes. "That's where I feel it too. There's medicine to help with that, you know. And counseling. Meditation. Things you can do."

I hand her a plate of potatoes and an omelet and chew a bite myself, gingerly, as if eating it slowly might not hurt my teeth, might make my stomach more accepting. "I guess I didn't know that the emptiness could just . . . I don't know . . . get deeper and deeper. I assumed there was an end to it. I've learned one thing, which is that one should never assume anything. Sometimes I missed Kay, if that's possible. I didn't literally miss her, but I missed her in the abstract. As in, there were a few nights here and there where I wanted a mother. Someone to hold me and sing lullabies. And you. I missed you."

She chews more slowly, wondering, perhaps, if I can be believed. Then she nods.

"I know you haven't forgiven me."

"You never asked." She tilts her head at me, questioning. "I missed you. For a couple of years. I wondered how you were doing. Sometimes I was angry. You never called or texted or emailed, and so I stopped waiting. I stopped looking out the window, hoping to see a truck pull up and you jump out. I wasn't angry, either, till you showed up. You became dead to me, I guess. So it's weird to see you again. It was . . . tough. To see you."

"Yes. Thank you."

She finishes her breakfast, stands up to clear her plate into a bucket that says ChiKEN SCRapS on it with marker in kid handwriting. "I guess that's the only thing I really want to know. I mean, I have a million questions. But if I only got one, I would like to be clear on how long. What's your plan here? What about this fire? We need to talk about this."

The coffee must be kicking in, my head is clearing. "The honest truth, Libby, is that I'll be going soon. There is trouble . . . I didn't know that when I came here. Honestly. I just thought that I didn't find the *pollos*, and so I came here, and then my plan was to see you for three or so days, and then disappear again."

"Where?"

I pause. Shrug. "I don't know. I guess it depended on how things went here. I guess I needed to see if I had a home. But now you and Ed know about the fire. I just don't know . . . There are things . . . I can't really put words to them . . . How guilty am I? I don't even know. I was supposed to pick up a group of people. I couldn't find them. They started a signal fire. That fire is out of control. I don't know what that *means*. But I'm not staying much longer. I wanted to come to say good-bye. Out of love. And respect. And, well, this is the hard one for me. To ask forgiveness."

"Okay, then." Her voice is very soft, and she looks above my head, deciding something, and then back at my eyes. Here we are, two sisters, staring at one another. Simple, real, open. "You don't exactly deserve this, Tess," she says. "I think there's probably more to the story. But I do have a secret. Something real. A surprise for you." Her smile is sad, but still she winks and stands up. "Ed will tell you all about it. And show you. Because I want to be here when Amber wakes up. So that we can talk. For real. Without you here. Because she is my first priority. About whatever she is feeling about you and your return. But Ed is going to tell you something. And Tess? I hope you're worthy."

Chapter Twelve

Ed eats his breakfast standing, leaning against the kitchen counter, and says seriously but also playfully, knowing he'll annoy me, "I'm grateful for the chickens who gave us the eggs, for the sun and water, for the wheat and corn that fed the chickens, for the earth that provided the nutrients for this particular potato, for the space here to make our own food, and to you for making it, Tess." When I smile, he adds, "And that is not all goofy crap. That is real gratefulness. Now, Tess, let's take a walk."

"Well, is that negotiable? I don't feel so good—" I'm not going to tell them about Alejandra. That she was in the group I was to pick up. That she likely started the fire. That she is gone. I push it down deep, deep, so that I can have this final day. The time limit is the only thing that makes it possible.

"Nonnegotiable."

"I didn't actually sleep—"

"—It will be about a mile. I'll bring water. I have something to show you. Something important. You owe us that much. One walk."

I glance toward Libby for confirmation that I need to do this, but she's doing dishes, purposefully avoiding my gaze. I wander over to the door, where shoes are stacked, and lace up some of her tennis shoes. The blisters on my feet haven't yet healed, and they'll open back up now, but it doesn't matter.

Ed sets his plate on the counter, escorts me out the door, and guides me west, toward the distant and hazy mountains. He lifts his ballcap off, pushes the glasses to his face, runs his hand through his sandy-curly hair. The sky is brilliant blue, the grasses turned into a dry-golden, the row of cottonwoods even more golden.

"Not so smoky today," I venture, look at him sideways.

"No."

"Maybe it's calming?"

"No. Just checked. Moving fast. I would prefer not to talk about this particular tragedy . . . at this particular time. There's nothing we can do at the moment. Except to say that all our actions have consequences, that everything we do puts a chain of events into action, and for that reason, Tess, we have to be careful. We have to be aware and careful."

"But sometimes a person has to stand up and make a choice. Make a firm decision and act. Not knowing if it's the right thing for sure. Hoping, though."

"Yes."

"And sometimes that person is wrong. Accidentally makes the wrong choice."

"Yes."

"You don't talk as much as you used to. I remember you being a weird-talker. All philosophy, in stops-and-starts and looping in weird directions. I remember the first time Libby and I met you, when we walked into Ideal Grocery to buy candy after high school let out, and there you were, pulling into the parking lot in your orange VW bus, and Libby said something like, *There's two kinds of folks around here, the ranching kind and the escape-people-hippie kind, and this dude is that second kind,* which just proved to be true, because we saw you unloading boxes of bottled honey to sell."

"You have a good memory." He waves his arm aimlessly in the air. "Look. Last night's wind took down so many leaves." It's true: the blooms of yellow that had been floating in trees are now on the ground, where they're floating in a different way. The cottonwoods still have leaves waving like small flags, triumphant that they're still holding on. "Amber comes out here. She likes climbing them. If I remember right, you used to talk a lot *less*. You've been surprisingly talkative."

I glance up at the spread of branches along an old creek bed that's dried up, the trees being the evidence of the ancient paths of water.

He pushes his glasses up on his nose and keeps walking. After a while, he says, "We're going to the house I lived in when I first met your family." He adjusts his glasses. "That house I lived in back when you were here last. I don't know if you know this, but I had lived in El Salvador for a while. In a small village in rebel-controlled territories, worked with the FMLN. I wanted to do something that mattered, so that *I* would matter. I snuck in solar-powered generators for radios. It's a long story, there was a solidarity movement in those days . . . Anyway, in the end, I just got my heart broken."

"By a woman?"

At this, he laughs sincerely. "That's exactly what Libby asked me when I told her this story. No, not by a woman. By everything else. Because I wanted to make a difference, and I realized I wasn't helping much, or maybe I was, who knows, but I felt so small. Maybe it was the first time I'd realized how much suffering there was, and my efforts were so minor compared to what someone with power could do."

The wind blows a little, Tess feels the shift in her hair.

She'll miss that.

The grass rolls like waves.

She'll miss that too.

The clouds boiling up over the mountains. They'll mean-
der this way, toward Tess, toward the plains.

They'll release hail or rain or lightning, or, more likely,
only drift on past.

Ed glances at me, sideways. "So I moved out here. So that I could feel like enough again. I needed to be invisible for a while. Just like you do, as the *levantona*. That's a real trick. The balance between being seen and unseen. *Pollos* need to be unseen so that they can start a new life and *not* be invisible. Acquire enough substance to build a life. But because they're trying to be invisible, they're not. Do you know, for example, that most of the immigrants get nabbed because of routine traffic stops? And did you know that most of those were caught by *la migra* on Highway 160, between Durango and Alamosa? The INS agents know it, and so do the *coyotes*. So why, I wonder, were you there?"

I breathe in, glance sideways. "It's not the INS anymore. It's ICE."

He sighs, annoyed. "I know that."

"They go north now. They go back roads, into Utah, then over. I-70. Drug drops right in Mormon territory. Right where you'd least expect it. But this group, I don't know. I was told to go there. An old spot we used to use——"

"Tess. Stop. I'm asking. Was anything about this pickup special?"

I shake my head, no.

He looks at me, genuinely curious. "You didn't know who the pickup was?"

I shake my head, no again. The shaking causes the world to spin, and the leaves that are falling seem to be falling in three dimensions, a spiral within a spiral.

Seasick is what I feel like. I look down, hoping to find my landfeet, looking for grounding. The sun is deafening now. I kick at a couple of leaves, sending them springing into the air.

"I built this house——" and here, he waves his hand at a structure I see in the far distance. "I built it by hand. By myself. One adobe brick at a time. Had no idea what I was doing. Learned as I went. Back when I was hurting and needing to feel again."

I give one good kick to a clump of grass underfoot. "You seem . . . good now."

"Emotions come back when you get calm enough to let them."

He scratches his jaw, stops, looks down, bends over and picks up a globe of what looks like gray tissue paper. "Wasp nest. They chew up leaves and bark and spit it out, and look what they make." He looks up at the cottonwood, where I suppose this was once sitting, the whole time balancing it gently in his palm, the fingers curved up around, holding it. Gray and hollow, like a skull.

I reach over and poke at the nest. How soft it is, as if maybe it's made from barely-hanging-together dust.

He glances over at me, keeps walking, looking off into the distance. He holds the wasp nest in one hand, like a god holding the globe of the earth. "The empty isn't going to fill up like magic, Tess." He stops, looks at me. "And it doesn't fill up with drink and drugs, either. It fills up by having a purpose. At least spend some time with Amber. Just for her sake, fake it. Do not break that kid's heart."

I shake my head, no.

"Well, when you do leave, look her in the eye. Say goodbye. And make her understand, in her heart, that you're not leaving because of her. Okay? You got that?" He looks at me until I nod. "You could lose your family for real, you know. I'm not sure you've ever considered that. You left and you've been gone, and I'm guessing that all this time, you took it for granted that they'd still be here. If this shit ever hit the fan. Which it has. Be careful, Tess. What you do or say next . . ." He sighs. "Whatever you do next will have big consequences. Please be careful. Please try to think beyond yourself."

I won't let him catch my eye, and so he tosses the nest gently to the ground and points toward the structure that has just come into view again. It's a small round home, stucco on the outside, another Earthship, but smaller and plain. Like the other, it's surrounded by a dirt driveway and a line of trees and a few little outbuildings. "This is what I want to show you."

"You still have that orange VW bus? Parked out here? That's what you had when *I* lived here."

As we near, Ed touches my shoulder and turns me to him. It startles me, and I pull back, but he pulls me close again, gently. He waits until I look him in the eyes. "Friends stay here now." He squeezes my shoulders, tight. "It's funny. How bits of people gather in us. Isn't it? Listen. One thing. It's one thing to be invisible. And another to be *un pelagato*—a nobody. It's a fine line. It's as fine as the dust of that wasp nest. Fine as each layer. Nobody is a *pelagato*. Nobody, not one single human, is a nobody."

He wants something from me, so I nod. Yes. Fine. Yes.

"Do you understand? So treat yourself, and treat them, like the invisible people you currently need to be. Invisible, but not a nobody. You understand the difference?"

The intensity of his voice makes me realize that what he's saying is as essential as my heartbeat. My face flushes. I look toward the home and realize something is out of whack. There is laundry. A pump with a small puddle of water on the ground. A group of chickens that scatter away. Then I make out a few people, who move inside as soon as they see us, except one. A young woman with a ponytail of the finest black hair. A startled face. The bloom of a smile.

Chapter Thirteen

My stomach caves, and I'm trying for oxygen between heaves. Ed is catching me underneath my armpits as I fall with a *whoa now* and he is dragging me over to a tree, which he leans me against once he's got me in the shade. Before I can suck in air again, there are arms wrapped around me and *lo siento, ay, lo siento*, and a wet cloth, and Ed's hand on my forehead.

It can't be.

My eyes dart at Ed, back to a young woman's startled face. She's grown up now, a woman, the curves of her face defined into sharper angles.

Ed whispers something at me, and it startles me enough to send me back against the tree bark. "Feel it, Tess. That swoosh of the heart. *That's* life. That is worth living for."

Alejandra.

I lean forward, my head between my legs. They are alive. I look up and bring them into focus. Alejandra. Now the age I was when I left here, smiling timidly at me, crooked eyeteeth, and there is Lupe, her mother, soft hands, as soft as a wasp nest, fluttering across my face.

Behind them is a cluster of men—about five of them—and I am hearing, *the fire, we were scared, we were alone,* and then I see it in Lupe's expression: they think I'm angry.

Alejandra, longglossyblackhair Alejandra, dimpleandcrookedeyeteeth Alejandra.

She puts out her arms to hold me.

I let out a moan that is not me. It is a moan of the universe.

Déjà vu: Me looking at Libby across the parking lot, wanting to put my arms out but not sure she would be that forgiving.

"*No nos odies por el fuego.* We thought we were going to die," Alejandra says as she nears, holds my eyes in hers. "It was that close." Her voice is fluid, and her eyes are steady. "We were so thirsty. We were dying. I started the fire so someone would *see* us. It was small. Oh, Tess. We put on dried branches for the smoke. I thought it would go out. We had waited for the pick-up person. We didn't know it was to be you. *No nos odies por el incendio que causamos . . .* We called one last number, then we called the police to turn ourselves in." She tilts her head slightly at Ed. "The only other number we thought we could call. The one you taught me, Tess."

"*No entiendo.*" The world starts spinning again, and I tilt over, and Ed holds me against the tree, mumbles something, touches my forehead. Then I am being held by Alejandra. Rocked by someone. Someone is feeling my pulse, touching my neck, touching my forehead. "You have a fever," Ed is saying quietly. "A high fever."

I close my eyes to bring the scattered bits together. I look to Ed first.

"Why didn't you *tell* me?"

He bends down, looks at me in the eyes, waits until I hold his gaze. "We were waiting to see what your plans were. What you were doing here, what you were about."

"I don't understand."

"We crisscrossed. You were on the bus here, and I was on my way there. Do you see? I had been driving like a maniac to the mountains. I didn't know about the fire either, that it was blazing into *that* fire, not until you told me."

Behind him, murmurings. "*Por favor, Tess, perdónanos. No nos odies por el fuego, nos estábamos muriendo de sed.*"

Lupe walks forward, takes my hand. "*No íbamos a vivir más que un par de horas.*" Her voice is flat. "*Teníamos tanta sed. Encendimos el fuego.*" She turns and walks away, limping.

Alejandra's voice is the opposite, full of calm kindness. "*Ay, Tess, no sabíamos que ibas a ser tú quien nos encontrará.* We had to leave the *mota y coca.* It's all burned. That man is going to be very angry."

I close my eyes. The world is getting dark. I hear a voice, my own voice. "But I can't understand this . . ."

"We were dying. Mama's leg—"

I hear my voice, but I am far away from it, in another world altogether. "I didn't know it was you, Alejandra. But I was looking. Waiting and waiting. And you never came. Forgive me. I was there. I looked. I waited and I waited."

"When we got to the road, Ed was there."

I close and open my eyes. I am sitting with a group of humans outside a small home, under the trees, in this huge expanse of a universe. Flies are buzzing around, and the sun filters through the yellow cottonwood leaves. I sip water from the glass in my hand.

"The color of the desert, the color of the land. That's how we were dressed, because that's how you survive. It was hotter, much hotter, than it is right now. One of the Lobo's *coyotes* was in the tallest building in Morales, watching the Border Patrol walk back and forth, and he had two more guys on the ground, watching as well, so that they could communicate, by radio, the—"

"Coordinates."

"Yes." She smiles at me but looks concerned. "In this way, they helped us cross the scariest part. The one hundred yards of barren land between the Mexican side and the U.S. side. We were on our stomachs. We did exactly as they said. 'Five meters forward. Stop. Okay, go. Stop. Down, stay down. Man looking your way. Down, down. It's gonna be a few hours, man. The guys are chatting. Rest. Fast, go five more.'"

"Oh, Alejandra—"

"Never did we raise our heads. Even when we had to—"

"Yes, I know."

"We only raised our heads to drink from the water bladders we each had on our backs. Enough to swallow. In this way, on our stomachs, we crossed one hundred meters of dry desert. Try to imagine, try to imagine moving so slow." She closes her eyes, and I do too, listening from the place of darkness beneath my eyelids, letting the red seep in. "Once we'd made it to the U.S. side, at the first vegetation, we could get to our hands and knees. Even though we had padded our knees and put on gloves, it was painful. Finally, we saw it, the small ditch, the blue Toyota—how happy we were to see the blue Toyota! It was another of Lobo's men. We climbed in, went to a house, and it was dark and horrible for days. It made us wish again for the sky and earth. We could hear a race track. The horses, the loudspeaker, the crowd. Such a gamble. Such a gamble, all of our lives are. Out there was food, water, life. But we stayed inside, and it is there that the money was delivered, four thousand dollars each, paid partly by your friend—"

"Slade?"

"Yes, Slade. We knew we were a surprise for you. We also had to carry *mota* and *coca*. I didn't want to, Tess. Then we were driven to a small road west of Alamosa. Lobo's man said, 'Wait here, wait exactly here.' So we did. We waited and waited. But there was no water in the creek where usually there is water. And so we moved.

Directly to the west, only one rise of a mountain, one day of hiking, because there was a stream of water, and then we walked back. We took turns leaving one person at the pickup spot."

"Oh, Alejandra—I must tell Slade. I must somehow tell him. He'll be so happy you're alive—"

"The cell phone had no reception. Only if we walked to the road. And so I did, and I called Lobo, but no one answered. We knew then we were alone. Then Mama fainted. And then I lit the signal fire, I did it." Here, tears rush out of her eyes. "We had no water to put it out, only a rock, but we did a good job. Then the wind started rising. I worried, but I thought it was out." Alejandra's tears turn to weeping, now, loudly. I touch her shoulder and then pull her into my lap. I glance at Lupe, whose leg is in a splint of sorts, the work of Libby, I can tell, the very way she wraps Kay's bandages. When my eyes travel up from Lupe's legs to her eyes, I see how dead they are, how this ordeal has been too much for her, too much open space, too much dark, too much fire. She has shut down, and I recognize it.

"*Hay más* . . . just so much more." Alejandra sucks in her breath and glances at me, her mother, back at me. "One of the men was bitten by *un cascabel,* while on his stomach, drinking. From the poison, he got so weak . . ."

"*Es demasiado,* it's too much, too much." Lupe's voice is a broken mumble, an empty not-right mumble. Despair that is beyond despair, dead that is beyond dead. "*Demasiado,* too much." She says it over and over, blurring the words together in English and Spanish. One of the men goes to her side and rocks her.

"So we waited, Tess. I daydreamed it would be you. I daydreamed that I was a little girl, and it was you again, pulling up in the truck, saving us from the desert. It had been so hard, and I prayed that it would get better. I prayed to the sky, and to the sand, to the earth . . ." She trails off and then leans against me, takes my hand. "And you didn't come. We heard a car honking, and we heard someone yelling, but it was far away, and we couldn't tell in what direction. The mountains are so large, Tess. People forget that. They are big. There's not always water . . ." She trails off, glances at the sky. "We had three tortillas for the all of us. One gallon of water for all of us. We found *piñones,* and raspberries, and *escaramujos.* But it was not enough, and we were already sick. And one morning, I woke up, and I knew we were *completamente solitos.* I just knew that the person was no longer out there, looking for us. No one was coming. Ever."

She stops until I nudge her, an old joke from when she was younger and was supposed to be telling me stories to keep me awake while driving.

She smiles a sad smile. "We were going to die. I could feel the sickness getting into all of us. I decided to build a signal fire and call 911. Even if we were deported, we'd be alive. Perhaps I wasn't thinking correctly. People forget that the brain doesn't work well when it's tired and hungry—"

I let out a laugh. "I do know."

Lupe looks at me, now calmed. "*Danos la paz.* Grant us peace."

Alejandra tilts her head at her. "Mama wasn't going to last much longer. I hiked until I had reception, and I called 911. And then I called Salvador." She breathes in, starts again. "I told him where we were. He didn't want to come. He said, 'I'm not doing that anymore,' but I explained, I begged. *Es un milagro* his number worked. The same number, after all these years."

"But the fire?"

"I walked back to the group. I smelled smoke. It had gotten windy. Clouds were coming. Then—aye! The fire jumped out of the little pit we had dug, but it was very small, and we put it out. We stamped and we threw rocks and dirt . . . and then, well, Ed was there, calling for us, and so we ran to his orange van, and I did not know his name was Ed, and it was just an orange blur, sitting there. That one moment was . . . what is the word? Heaven. But at the same time, the fire was starting."

Ed sits next to me. Nudges me with a water bottle. "I didn't realize you knew these people. Until I picked them up, and on the drive here, in my bus, they started asking careful questions. They knew someone from out this way. They knew a dark-haired beautiful girl. Who had given them my phone number." His voice is soothing, but it sounds far away, as far away as a hundred yards of desert. He is facing Alejandra and Lupe and the group of men. "Tess, you're sick. Stay here. I'll come back with the truck. I don't want to make you walk back. I don't want to drive the VW right now—I just used it for . . . this. Just rest here. Later, when you see Amber, don't tell her. About any of this. In all other ways, we try to be honest. But not this. Secrets are burdens."

I nod. Yes. I know secrets are burdens.

A sudden burst of noise startles us all. A mariachi band. It takes me a moment to realize that it's the ringtone on Ed's cell. And as he fumbles for it, and answers it, I claw out of my fog. My fog of this story—their story and my story. I'm too tired, and it seems too much: Alejandra and Lupe and their cousins, all rescued, all not burning. All here. With a future.

From Ed's phone, I can hear the tone and pitch of Amber's voice: *Please come now. It's Kay.*

Ed holds the phone to his stomach, looks at me, reaches his hand to pull me up, decides otherwise. "You can't make it. I need to run." His voice is firm. "You stay here. Do you understand? I'll come back." With that, he starts back to the farmhouse, speaking into the phone as he goes.

I watch him jog away from us, heat waves on the earth spiraling up to make him warp, make the landscape warp, and I feel my heart finally warp too. Finally, finally. Finally it has lost its beat, its rhythm.

Finally it is giving up. I wince, pull into my mind the picture of Amber sleeping, Alejandra's smile, Slade with arms outreached, of my sister taking a step toward me.

*

Time flows like water, like wind, like air. Perhaps hours, perhaps minutes. I wake and drink water and shift around to the other side of the tree, where Lupe and Alejandra already have moved themselves for the shade.

> Only some people know how important shade is,
> comforting, consoling, lifesaver.

> Tess takes Alejandra's hand in one, Lupe's in another.
> Three women, sitting under a tree, holding hands in
> silence. Something inside them shifting around.

> Tess wonders if she can hold the different parts of herself
> and bring herself back together.

> There is real talking to be done.
> Too bad humans can't whistle the huge truths.

I watch a leaf laugh its way down, passing tenderly through time and space, and I remember the last time I saw Libby and Amber before I left:

> —Infant Amber was sleeping in her car seat outside in the shade,
> —and she was rocking her head, back and forth, just coming out
> of a sleep,
> —and her eyes drifted open and stared up at me,
> —and she made a movement, then, kicking her arms and legs, like
> she was running with joy.

—Behind her, Libby was painting our old house, and she had
bought fifteen gallons of light purple paint, and I knew then,
with that color choice, that she was making the decision to
make a good and real life for herself.

—And I was sorry. Sorry because I knew, when I left, that we
would talk of smaller and smaller things. We would go backward, from love to not-knowing.

—She looked down from the ladder and said, Tess, it's rude to
stare, but on the other hand, in order to see, you have to keep
looking. Go ahead and stare. Keep looking at them, at people.

*

We doze. Then I awake to murmur, "Which one? Which one of those
boys is your *novio?*"

But she turns to me. "His name was Oscar. He—"

I can feel the knowledge in her, that every fiber of her being has
been worn out, nearly to extinction, and I understand, too, that her
boyfriend had burned up. He had died of poison, of snakebite, then
burned. I take her hand and pull her to me and rock her like a child.
Two of us under a tree, in the sparse shade, rocking.

*

Time shifts, blends with earth and sky. Later, she starts up again. Her
words land in my mind, circle around, a bird in flight. "I didn't know
you had a sister, a daughter, this, how do you say it? *Cuñado*, brother-in-
law," she says. "You never said . . . that part. You only told me, when I
was a girl, to call this number if ever I was in trouble. Remember how
you made me memorize it? But you never told me who it was. *Salvador*.
That's what you called him, that's what we called him."

I nod. Lick my lips. Stare at the sky.

She sighs. "Remember when I was a child. I was . . . how do you say it? Annoyed at you. For making me memorize that number."

"I remember," I say, leaning my head back against the tree. "He stopped doing this work, you know. Because he had married Libby——"

"Yes, and adopted your Amber. But I had memorized his phone number. Long ago, when I was a girl." She looks at me, touches my chin so that I have to look at her. "You saved my life. You came to me, on the mountain, with that phone number. And hours later, a man arrived in an orange van. I did not know that he was related to you. We only hoped to be saved. But on the way here, across the fields of Colorado, *aprendimos*. He knew the color of your eyes. You saved us."

"I've never saved anyone." But it is a whisper, and she doesn't hear it.

"It was a small fire. There were storm clouds building, and then it started to rain. And I was so relieved. I thought it was God, sending us a gift. And so we got in the VW, and we came here. I never knew . . . about wind, about the . . . wind and air and the earth. I just hope you are not too angry."

"You have no idea how happy I am to see you, happy you're alive." I whisper this to her and lean over, put my head onto her stomach. "I never told you I'd given birth to a baby. But I had, and then I left. I left my baby with my sister. And I became a *levantona*. I knew Ed back then, a little. I knew he was a kind man, doing the same work, but for different reasons." Suddenly I laugh, an odd sound issuing from my throat.

Lupe is reciting the Lord's Prayer. "*Padre nuestro que estás en el cielo . . .*"

We murmur it along with her, an old habit. When we are done, Alejandra touches my shoulder. "What about that man? Slade? Your *novio*?"

"Well, he's never quite been my *novio*."

"*Ay, dios mío.*" She says this disapprovingly. "But he's liked you for so long. Back and forth you two go. Just *decide,* Tess. Decide to go for it. Loud up your heart."

I smile. Our old conversation, relived. "He's at the old house, the one I grew up in. He brought you here. He paid your way as a gift to me. *Ay, mija,* we need to tell him you're alive."

Chapter Fourteen

I stand in the middle of NoWhere, Colorado, my homeland. In front of me is the podunk crummy house that held the enormity of my childhood; at my feet is a red cooler with a smashed red bow on top. I open it up and see that Slade has provided well for me, offered up my version of frankincense and myrrh: Seagram's 7, 7 Up, a plastic cup, some pot, aspirin, and a note. *Worried about you. Drove by Libby's and Kay's looking for you this morning. Was discreet and didn't stop—but want to check on you. Don't do anything stupid. Drove up to the reservoir. You know the direction I'll be at. Worried I might be seen here. I'll spend the day up there. Gonna fish. I threw away my cell phone, didn't want any way to be tracked. No way to reach me, I'll be back. Be there with your family. It's a good idea. Chin up. Together we'll figure out the next steps.*

I pour myself a drink and sit on the cooler, hold my hot head to my hands, and glance at Ed's orange VW bus that got me here. Something about the purple of the house, the orange of the bus, the blue of the sky makes my head spin. I should go check on Kay, I should find Slade to tell him the news. But the Seagram's and 7 Up sliding cool down my hot throat, the yellow leaves, the white puffs of cloud, turquoise sky.

Oh, universe, thank you. Alejandra is alive. Really, that is something. All of them: Libby, Amber, Lupe, Alejandra—all alive, and each of them has someone, they have family, and, yes, really, that is something. I stare at the old house, a small violet square in a vast expanse of fields. From here I can see the rusted-out cars. The bird-bath Kay used as a cigarette tray. The burn barrel where once I saw the streamers floating out with the WELCOME HOME TESS AND BABY AMBER sign that Libby had made in her lastditch effort to keep me around. The rise of a windmill and a few trees near which a hawk circles.

The memories flood. There I am on the day we moved in: a skinny-legged young kid in jeans and a red T-shirt standing at the threshold of the house, afraid to walk in the door of this new and dark place. Kay walking by me, carrying cardboard boxes from the bed of the pickup, mumbling about leaving our old life behind, starting a new chapter in a place where the bills could be met and she could finally relax.

There is Libby, my big sister, saying, *Come, Tess, come look at these purple flowers, come look at the barn, it's all empty and abandoned! Come look at these barrels where you burn trash! Come look!*

There I am, later in the day: cautious and watching an old man with blue eyes and white hair poking from a ballcap introducing himself as Baxter. I wander by so I can listen to him discussing with Kay the details of the deal, free rent in exchange for work as a ranch hand. Libby is at my side, whispering. *See that big farmhouse across that field? That's where that man lives. He's our landlord. He owns this ranch. He has cows over in a far pasture. We can pet them!*

There I am, new backpack and shoes, standing at the doorway of this house, afraid to step from the dark cool out into the hot morning for my first day at a new school that has PIRATES as its mascot. There I am the next year and the next, new backpack, new shoes. Older. Year by year. Marked only by sharp points: the time I broke my arm, the time Libby's cat died, the time Kay was covered in vomit and pee and Libby said, *I'm not sure we should drink when we get older.* The time Kay dated the guy with the eyepatch, the time she dated the one with the motorcycle, the time she dated no one and drank even more. The rest is a blur. Of breakfasts. Of homework. Of running through alfalfa fields. But mostly a blur of fear. Why, Tess, why? Because my voice would not work. Words would not come. My body was too small. The world was too loud, the screaming too sudden, the wall too hard, the slaps too stinging, the choking too tight.

There were no words that could protect me.

But, yes, there were.

Libby's sharp voice: *That's enough, Mom. Leave her alone.*

Baxter's low growl, *You'll be leaving now and not be coming back*, to a boyfriend of Kay's, and then Baxter turning to Kay with fury in his eyes and saying, *That's enough of that now. You'll be leaving that life alone.*

They found the words. I raise a toast to Baxter and to Libby.

And then to Kay, who in all those years was lonely and strungout and surprised by the stupidity of life. Now her time is up. Her clock is stopping. I raise my glass and murmur a toast to the stars, whose cold distraction only confirms my suspicion that they long ago disassociated from the warmth the world had to offer. I wish they would come back and give us another try.

*

And wouldn't you know it, but there is Kay, sitting in her chair, her seagreen eyes flaring at me. Is that possible? That I'm standing above her all of a sudden? Is that my voice? Did I really fling my drink into the grass? Put down the cup? Walk over here?

Is that really her in front of me, working so hard to breathe? Is that her face, skin pulled so tight over bone? Are those her hands folded over her belly that once housed me? Are those her eyes, softening? Kay, Kay—

Can you help me? Can you help me understand?

Because I feel only half here, but I can't find the other half.

You birthed me. But you birthed an unwhole human. Where is the rest of me?

Did you witness its departure? Can you help me get that part of me back?

I'm asking you for real.

I was hoping you might know.

I keep sweeping my heart, looking for the missing piece. Which corner is it in?

Tess, Tess— I didn't, I couldn't— Try to understand—

Kay— And now you're leaving? What gives you that right? You need to fix things first. You need to make some things right. Clean up your mess. Please help me find the missing piece.

Tess, Tess—

The missing piece. It's there. I see it.

If anyone can see it, I can. We had much in common. That's how I know.

You'll find it sooner than I did.

You'll find it soon. You're nearly there.

PART IV

Air

Chapter Fifteen

I open my eyes to Libby's face, and I gasp for air. My throat burns. I close my eyes to go back into the dark. Open them, blink, gasp. Our eyes meet across a great distance though she is right in front of me. Deepdoebrown eyes. She is saying something, and I hope her breath sends oxygen into my body. I gasp to suck in her air. I want her oxygen to fling itself into my body. I feel the ache of my heart and the thumping of my head. I feel my bones scratching to get out.

*

I open my eyes because some voice is demanding I do so. It's a man this time, olive skinned, wire-framed glasses circling dark eyes. "You will wake up now, miss. You're in the hospital. Can you hear me? Can you tell me your name? Wake up now."

I look at him and nod, but my mouth forms no words, and there is not enough air. My hands fly like birds to my face, but there are plastic tongs in my nose and he is guiding my hands back down. "Let that be," he says. The side of my face feels bulky and swollen, my mouth feels like cotton. I close my eyes to calm the terror. My ears seek out noises to place me: a nearby motor clicking, the screech of a cart far away, the hiss of fluorescent lights, the burst of an intercom, a man's voice, the squeak of a door, the boom of my pulse in my ears.

He leans closer. "Wake up."

*

Later, I wake. He is talking to me again, and I keep my eyes closed, but I hear fragments: "Could even be sepsis, from that infection in your mouth. We'll have all the blood work back soon to confirm."

Then, to someone else, "Her blood pressure was low and her heart rate was up. We have the basic lab work, but we need the rest. It will be in soon."

Directed back at me: "Miss? Can you open your eyes? I wonder if you have had abdominal pain and difficulty breathing? Have you been vomiting? You are anemic. We have blood cultures pending. Can you understand me? Can you tell me your name?"

*

Later, I wake. I open my mouth, but the ache is too great. I close it gently. There are no words anyway.

Again, the man is beside me. "I have you on a broad-spectrum antibiotic via IV. We need the cultures back before I decide what to do next. I also believe you've been hard on your body. General malnutrition." When I look up at him, hazyeyed, he nods to a plastic bag hanging from a metal hanger. "Do you see that? That is what we call a 'banana bag,' which is vitamins and minerals." He reaches out and turns my face toward him. "Your sister just left. She will be back. You're going to feel better now."

I try to drift off, but he shakes me awake.

His face softens. "Your sister is a friend of mine. She says . . . Well, I do believe that perhaps your life has not been so easy of late, miss. I do think that perhaps now it will get better." It's his tenderness that brings tears in my eyes, which he notes, and he reaches out to touch my shoulder.

*

Later, I wake. He is at the foot of my bed, talking with Libby. I close my eyes so I can just listen.

I hear, *Blood work is in. The oral antibiotics now is fine. We can take out the IV.*

I hear, *She must have been feeling quite terrible.*

I hear, *The pain meds for her teeth are important. That must have hurt very much.*

I hear, *Release as late today as we can manage; bring her back in the morning for a checkup.*

*

I wake again to find the room empty, which seems a relief, and I stare at the ceiling until I hear a noise. "Is Kay sick? Did I somehow kill her?" The words fly out of me the moment Libby comes walking in the room, a handful of blooming purple alfalfa in one hand. She puts the bundle of blooms on the table next to me. It smells like only alfalfa can smell, the deep green, rich soil, hint of purple, and the opposite of what I feel, bonedry. "Don't be scared. The noise you hear is the heart monitor. There's also the IV pump for a bit yet. I'm sure your mouth hurts a lot. It's okay if you don't want to talk much. Kay is alive."

"Oh, Libby." My tongue is thick and my jaw aches with the movement. "I've gone crazy, haven't I?"

She leans toward me and takes my hand. "How do you feel?"

I brush her comment away with a lift of my hand, a small motion because of the tug of an IV. "I remember . . . sitting in the field, right near the old house. Remembering stuff about when we were young. I was sitting there, all these memories flowing into my brain, and I couldn't stop them—"

She reaches out to touch my forehead. "There I was, in the bathroom, getting hot towels, and suddenly you were at the doorway, asking questions and crying." She turns away from me. "Ed and Amber had just gone home to do chores. It was you and me and her. Do you remember? That she said she was sorry?" Libby moves back some of my hair. "She's at home. She's got an infection in her PICC line. She won't come in. She has a DNR. She's ready. I've called hospice to go out to the farmhouse, to help her with the pain."

I close my eyes. "Oh, I shouldn't have . . ."

Libby's voice gets thick, like her own throat is constricting. She turns away, wipes her face. "She apologized, Tess. I've never heard her say *I'm sorry*. But she did. To you, and to me. Tess, I think maybe Kay infected the PICC line on purpose. I saw a clamp. It wasn't threaded right. I think she pulled off the cap."

The intercom in the hallway blasts a call. There's the squeak of shoes, the murmur of voices. "Is there time? I want to tell her that I'm sorry too . . ."

"Well, yes. When they discharge you. Which they want to do before three PM. There should be enough time."

"And they did some tests?"

"You're not so healthy at the moment. Good thing Dr. Lemon is my friend. He was very thorough."

"His name is Dr. Lemon?"

"Everyone just calls him that because no one can pronounce his last name."

"What, one of those poor medical students who got assigned to NoWhere, Colorado, so that he can pay off his medical school bills?"

She smiles. "Yes, actually. Yes."

"My mouth really hurts."

"The dentist left before you woke up. Do you remember? I think they went ahead and put you under so they could work with your mouth. What a mess. Whoever pulled your tooth left in two roots, Tess, which became infected. She cut your gums and scraped out the infection. Try to leave it alone. "

"That's why it's puffy?"

"Yes."

"It hurts."

"Yes. I imagine it does."

"I feel hard pokey things . . ."

"Stitches. Leave them alone."

"Where's Amber?"

"At school."

"Not with Kay?"

"No. I wanted her to go today. You can check her out for me when you leave here." Libby leans over, takes my hand in hers. Our eyes, brown and deep and sorry, meet.

I take this in. "But Amber, she's okay?"

"She's fine."

"So, I spent one whole night here?"

"Yes."

"And I'm just now waking up?"

"You were pretty feverish."

"Is the fire still going?"

"Yes."

"Is it smoky out?"

"Yes. The news says it has spread . . ." She bites her lip. "The remains of one human have been found, a man believed to be a Mexican national. The trees are too dry, the wind too fierce."

"Oscar?"

"We think so."

"And Alejandra? Where is she?"

"She's safe, they're all safe." Then she glances around. "Don't talk about it here—" But then she smiles. "You taught them Ed's number?"

I reach up to touch her nose. "Long ago."

"Tess, there's something serious I need to ask you. Alejandra said that you left in the VW to go tell a man named Slade that they were safe. I need to know who he is." But then another nurse is there, wanting to draw blood, and then Dr. Lemon comes in, signing papers, so I look up at her and whisper, "Don't worry, I'll tell you later, I will." Then there is a wheelchair, and papers, and bottles, and instructions, and eventually I close my eyes and let it all happen to me. The human heart-puzzle is a hard one to put together, especially when you're missing a few pieces.

*

When Libby asks if I'm well enough to get Amber, I tell her that if I've got one ability, it's that I can keep going when the going gets tough. I pull into the school parking lot and sit in the shade and make a list.

 —ONE: PICK UP AMBER AT SCHOOL

 —TWO: TELL KAY GOODBYE

 —THREE: TELL SLADE ALEJANDRA IS ALIVE

 —FOUR: BE WITH AMBER, ALEJANDRA, LUPE

 —FIVE: AFTER DOING ALL THE ABOVE, FIGURE OUT
   WHAT TO DO. I CAME HERE FOR THREE DAYS AND
   AN EXIT PLAN. NOT SURE WHERE TO GO NEXT.

I tuck the list in my jeans and walk into my old school, the HOME OF THE PIRATES flag flapping above my head as I do. Holymoley, you'd think things would change over time, but they do not. The same lost-and-found table right up front with sweatshirts and gloves and lunchboxes. Gym, library, classrooms, and worst of all, the lunchroom, stupid kickball and sit-ups, but most of all the eating itself, the people who weren't there to sit next to, the shame.

Somewhere down to the left, where the elementary school is, I hear music—kindergartners clapping their hands, and the teacher yelling, *long-short-shortshort-long*! To the right, in the middle school, there are the sounds of squeaky shoes on the basketball court. Then there's a woman standing in front of me. "I'm sorry, but who are you? You can't go in. Are you here to volunteer? Dropping off some cans for the food drive?"

"I'm here to pick up Amber."

She looks me up and down, and I remember my middleschool manners and do the same. She clears her throat, rolls her eyes, a small moment of cruelty that she does on purpose. "Yes, Libby just called." She glances at the clock, picks up the phone, says, "Amber is being checked out," and soon enough, Amber comes walking up the hall, bright red backpack slung over her shoulder. She passes another girl in the hall, and she lifts her hand in a small wave, and the girl lifts her head, turns it slightly, rejecting it. I burst out in a sudden bark of a laugh. Such a small motion. Such a small heartbreak of a motion. Experienced by the both of us.

Amber walks up to me, red backpack swinging behind her, because, like all of us, she must go on. "Hi, Tess. You were sick. Are you okay?"

"Oh, okay," I say. Because it's just now hitting me: what I didn't see at home, what Ed and Libby haven't even seen. This kid's life isn't so easy here. Maybe compared to an immigrant crossing the desert, sure.

But she's a kid that gets teased: She's too different with her beekeeping-hippie parents and no-sugar household and Buddhist stuff—and she's bravely raising her chin to it all and pretending it doesn't matter, but it does, it does, and the fact of this is hitting me hard. "Oh boy, okay." I take the backpack from her, try to bring this moment back into focus. "Jeez, this weighs a ton."

"Our class won. Is your mouth okay? You just get out of the hospital?"

"Won what?"

"My class had the most food cans. For the food bank. How's Kay?"

"Libby sent me here. Kay is at home . . . It could be that . . . she's getting worse and that it's maybe happening faster than . . . Libby wanted you to be there."

Immediately tears fly into Amber's eyes, and what a beautiful thing to see, emotion so fluid and immediate and unfettered.

*

On the way out, I glance over at the same spot on the sidewalk where I was just a few days ago. Me, sitting with Libby. All this, in a few days? It seems impossible. Impossible that here I am, again, walking to the same pickup truck, now with my daughter instead of my sister, and the whole world seems to have done one strange miraculous circle.

I glance over at Amber before I pull out onto the road. "I guess you don't need me to tell you how stupid kids can be. That it gets easier. That middle school is the worst. Sounds like you know. But still . . . is it lonely? Is school . . . tough?"

"I don't care."

I glance at her, raise an eyebrow, and because she doesn't add anything, I add, "When I was about your age, well, that was the first time I got called a slut." I pull out of the parking lot, drive through town, toward the highway. "But I wasn't, of course. Libby was older, and she'd come by and check on me at lunch. Libby was just born with the need to protect. I'm sorry if sometimes you feel alone."

She's looking out the window, away from me. By now we're away from town, fields surrounding us in every direction, burnt yellow with the sun. Once in a while, there's a windmill and a stock tank and a couple of cows. Everything is so far apart here. Maybe that's why I became a *levantona*. Because I was used to driving long distances. We pass a piece of plywood leaning against a haystack that says WE HAVEN'T HAD ANY TRASPASSERS LATELY, and there's a skeleton propped against it.

"That's not funny," I tell her as we pass. "You okay? Something on your mind?"

"Kay says that dying is part of living," she says. "And that this culture is nuts. We're nuts because we're cowards. We spend zillions of dollars, and instead we should let death just happen. But she wasn't sure she'd be brave enough at the end."

A snort escapes me. "That's true for most of us, I think."

She clears her throat. "Hey, Tess? What about *your* friends? Do you have any? Would they come visit *you*?" She looks genuinely curious.

I turn to her, search her eyes for a second before I look back at the road. "Naw. At the moment, I have no friends."

"Really? Are you done with your . . . work?"

"As a *levantona*? Yeah." And then, because she doesn't look settled, I add, "I'm done with that life."

"The fire." She turns her body enough so that she's facing me. She sucks in the top of her mouth. "Instinct," she says quietly.

I put on the blinker that takes us to Kay's house. Look at her, hard. "What are you saying?"

"Nothing." She looks out the window, away from me, out the window into a field of green winter wheat.

"I'm not supposed to talk about it with you, Amber. Otherwise I would."

"Fine."

"No, wait. You're right. We're talking about something real here." I reach out my hand to touch her shoulder, but she flinches away. "Amber? I'd like to talk to you more. I think I know what you're getting at. Trying to ask. But right now, well, we're here. Kay's not well. So let's take one thing at a time here. Kay is first on the list."

"Okay."

"I guess you haven't seen a dead body before. Except Baxter?" She doesn't respond, so I add, "It's gonna be weird, when she dies. Maybe it will be quiet and calm. But it might not be. It's okay—I'm sure you know this—but it's okay to decide not to be there."

She shrugs, like she doesn't need to hear it, and her hands take to braiding her hair. She has an extra barrette she doesn't need, and so she hands it to me, and I twist my bangs back and clasp it together. "Seriously, Amber. I wish someone had told me this. The thing about seeing difficult things is that those images are with you forever. I'm not saying we should turn away from life. But I think it's okay—it's a good idea—not to see certain things if we don't need to. It's like stepping really far away from a dangerous horse so you don't get kicked unnecessarily. When you see something, there it is. In your brain. You wake up every single morning of the rest of your life with a certain image in your head . . . I guess I'm just saying to be careful what you choose to witness. Okay?"

She nods, and I can tell her objection has softened, and then I can feel her mind working out what I've just said. "Have you ever seen a dead person?"

I breathe out. I want to tell the truth. But if I do, I put the same kind of image and knowledge in her head that I'm asking her to avoid. Middle Way. That's what Ed was saying the other day. I go for a half-truth. "I saw a human skeleton once. In the desert. It really bothered me, and it still does. I was curious, and so I stared at it for a long time. Which is maybe normal, or good, or a bad idea, or who knows. But it's true I wish that image wasn't in my head." A flash of other images comes flickering by, the other things I wish I could expel: Me getting fucked by men who didn't care, Lobo saying *Te voy a matar, pinche culero,* that red barrette in black silky hair, and that infant baby, ready to be born.

I pull up to the house, and before we get out of the truck, we turn to each other. I'd like to hold her hand, but she is holding herself apart. She is drawing into herself, pulling inward. I put my hand out, trying to bring her back, but she turns and walks ahead of me toward the house. If only I could protect her from the sorrow that's heading our way. That's something I'd like to do.

Chapter Sixteen

Kay has sunken into her bones. Her skin is gray, her body is ready. Libby is sitting in a chair near her head, Ed is at her feet, and they both have hands on her, heads bent, Ed murmuring some kind of Buddhist death chant. Kay's hands are placed over her stomach, and one of Libby's hands is moving slowly back and forth over them, soothing, the other on the crown of her head, soothing there as well.

"It's time to say goodbye to grandma." Libby says this to Amber in a quiet voice.

Amber reaches out for my hand, then. It surprises me, but I have the presence of mind to give her hand a small squeeze of thanks. We walk to the bed together. We can't see Kay's face until we get close, but once I do, I can see that death is near. Her eyes are open, and she's not tracking. There is a thick liquid in her mouth that puffs and bubbles with every breath. Her jaw makes a small circle, and I wonder if the woman in the desert did the same thing. It's these details that break your heart.

Libby swabs out her mouth and puts her hand on her forehead. Amber lets out a little moan, and Libby whispers to her, "I just had the hospice worker leave. The time has come. It will be easier for her to go if you're brave and peaceful now. It will help *her* be brave and peaceful. Hearing is one of the last things to go. So tell her anything you want to tell her."

Amber looks uncertain for a moment but then leans over Kay and puts her hands on Kay's cheeks. "Goodbye, Grandma. I wish your soul peace, I really love you, I am really glad you were my grandma, you were pretty much the craziest orneriest grandma anyone could have. I sort of doubt that if there is a God that he's going to put up with you, actually"—and here Ed chuckles sadly—"but I'll miss you, and you should know that. I won't ever forget you."

Ed leads Amber out. They've both said their goodbyes, and I know Ed is protecting Amber from the last bit, too. I turn to Libby. "Is she in pain?"

"I hope not. There's morphine to help—"

"Oh man, I can't—"

"You can." She gives me a hard look, tilts her head toward Kay.

I open my mouth, close it. Look at Libby, and I know, in that instant, that she will never forgive me, nor will I forgive myself, if I do not find some words. I clear my throat. Try again. "Kay. Mom. I just wanted to say goodbye. I just want to wish you peace too." I glance over at Libby, who looks relieved. Yes. I am doing this right. "Mom, I'm going to get my life together." There is no change in her expression—just the deep huffing and gurgling of her breath. "Mom. If you get a chance, tell Baxter hello. Tell him thanks for coming over to hang out with us. *He* was the guardian angel." I look around the room. I don't know what else to say. "Mom, I'm sorry I was a bitch sometimes, and I often feel that I can't forgive you for being a bitch sometimes. But we should try, huh? For each other? I think we got hard because there wasn't much to soften us up. I'm sorry. Maybe you set something in motion, but I'm the one who kept it going. I kept it going." I look at Libby, and she is crying softly. "And no matter what, I won't forget you. You're pretty unforgettable."

Kay starts gasping. She needs air. Even I can see that. I look around the room, as if seeking out extra oxygen, something that can inflate her lungs. Libby presses her hands more firmly onto Kay, holding her in this suffering, and I put my hands on Kay's arm and do as well.

Then there is quiet. I get up and open a window. Because all spirits should be able to fly out, free. Or to let in and out the air. I stare from Kay's body to the window, just wondering if perhaps I can see a wisp depart. There is nothing except two sisters in the startled silence.

*

Libby picks up the phone, and I bolt outside to pace back and forth. A few leaves sing their way down to the earth. It's breezy out and smells like it's rained somewhere far off and that the wind is blowing me that gift, of water-soaked air, although, underneath, I still smell the fire.

I look toward the old house, a square of purple. I start walking there, slowly, letting memories of Kay float around. The good ones, the bad ones. Doing puzzles at the table at night. Startling me with a yell. Standing over the stove. Head resting on the kitchen table, sleeping.

Slade's truck is not outside near the ditch. Only the red cooler I left there yesterday, so I continue on to the house. The door is unlocked, and I open it slowly and peek in. I haven't been inside this place for ten years. Never thought I'd return. I pause in the doorway and then step into the kitchen. It smells like mouse piss and dust, is cobwebbed and filthy, but I can see that at one time, Libby made the effort. The cupboards had been painted a bright yellow, curtains had been hung. I turn to the right and swing open the door to the bed-room Libby and I shared, separated by a sheet, which is still hanging down the middle. Now there's nothing in either half, but I remember how it was—hers half tidy and mine a mess.

I wander into the small main room and sit on the old couch, dust flying around me. Here is where Kay would sit, doing puzzles. Or having a drink. Here was where Libby and I would sit to watch TV. To do homework. Here is where I'd kiss boys I'd snuck into the house. Where the various dogs we had would crawl into our laps. Here was my life. Outside, the afternoon is turning to evening as clouds boil up. I doze, wish I could cry, doze again. I wake to the clouds closer, purplish, green, darker. Dark is coming, and I should get back to Kay's, or Libby's. I stand and look around one last time. "Goodbye, Kay."

At that moment, there is a flash of red. Then another. I jump up and stand at the door to see a police car pulling up. A man emerges from the driver side. My heart starts pounding, thick and heavy.

"That you, Tess?"

"I'm so sorry about the fire."

"What?" He walks over to me, shines a light above my head to cast enough light on my face. "You *are* Tess, right? You don't look like you used to—"

I'm not used to meeting an officer's eyes. I force myself to stay calm, to look, and I see it's Miguel, a friend in high school, a friend of Libby's. He shakes my hand, but then his hand goes back to his waist, resting on the shadow of what I assume to be a holster. "Where's Amber?"

"What?"

"Amber is missing."

"Well, she's probably off crying. Kay just died."

He shakes his head no. "I'm sorry for that. But Ed took Amber home, and went to feed the animals, and one of the heifers was out, so it took him a bit, and then he came back to the house and she was gone—"

I close my eyes, tight, and see the afterimage of the flashlight glow biting into the dark. I'm trying to squint into my brain, to peer there, to see if there are any answers or clues. I open them back up. "Honest to god, Miguel, I have no idea."

"Here's the thing, Tess. There were signs of a fight. Knocked-over chairs—"

I look beyond him at the moon. "So? Couldn't that just be a temper tantrum? Am I the only person around here that ever experiences those?"

"Maybe she did just run off. Upset. That's what I think." He pauses, looks around. "I remember this place," he murmurs quietly. "But Tess, your sister seems to think it's something else. Gut instinct, she says. We'd sure like to find her. You don't know anything?"

I pause. How to explain Slade? The fire? Alejandra? And the group of immigrants and Ed's role in getting them? Ed asked me not to, Libby asked me not to. It could bring all sorts of trouble. "She's not here."

He sighs, glances past me into the house. "I'm going to go in and do a search. Then I'll be heading back to Libby's house. Do you want a lift? Back to their house?"

No: the last thing I want to be is in a car with an officer. "I'll walk back to Kay's house, where I have the truck. There's no one here, but you should check."

He glances past me and raises his flashlight, stepping inside, but then turns to look briefly at me. He knows enough about what went on here; he knows it wasn't good; he knows I got pregnant, had a baby, and left and he has watched Libby raise Amber on her own; and likely he knows about my line of work. "Help your sister out, Tess. Let's find Amber."

I look into the darkening fields. "I can do that," and with that, I start jogging back to the home where my mother just died.

*

At the old farmhouse, I paw through the drawers. Sure enough, there are little bundles of cash in Kay's usual places—in her shoes, in her dresser. I check the other usual places—under the mattress, in the laundry room—but there's nothing. It looks like a coupla hundred dollars. Just in case.

Amber's probably cuddled up with one of her cows, right? Or she's just getting some damn space—probably Ed and Libby don't give her enough *room*. She's probably riding her bike down some country road. They don't understand how a person can flip out, be irresponsible, lose touch with the need to stay grounded and predictable. Probably Amber has that gene. From me. And it's just now taking hold.

I drive back to Libby's, and I'm surprised, when I pull in, to find four sheriff cars, lights going, so bright in the dark of the night. Libby comes running up to me. Ringo follows her and jumps up on me, scared or excited, scraping me with his claws all the way down my leg.

"You don't have her? You haven't seen her? She's not at the old house?" She's grabbing my shoulders, shaking. "She used to go there sometimes, too. She's not there? Are you sure?"

"No." My voice feels thick and foggy. "She's not there. What about at . . . Ed's old house? With Alejandra?"

"Oh, god." Libby is wildeyed. "What did you do? Who is Slade? Who did you *bring here*? He's got her. You need to *find her!*"

"Libby! Stop!" I paw away her hands, which are flying around my shoulders, trying to shake me, slap me. "Stop! I didn't do anything. She probably ran off to cry somewhere, you know? Her grandmother just died!"

Libby grabs my arms tight and pulls me to her. Her voice is blurhiss. "Alejandra and Lupe and everyone are gone. Gone! Ed drove over there first, figuring that Amber had walked over there for some reason. And the place is deserted. Where would they go?" She pauses, looks at me. "Tess, tell me. You always bring trouble. Damn you! I know you're involved in this somehow. Is there some *jefe* around here? If you— If you—" She shoves me, hard, and I go flying backward, falling on my ass. "Oh my god, I'm going to kill you," she's screaming. Now she's kicking me, and Ed is running over, holding her tight, and then there are cops, everywhere, holding her and looking at me, waiting for an answer.

The wind is coming up. Fast, hard, spraying dirt in our faces. The temperature is falling, fast, and spits of tiny hail shutter down from the sky. Everyone ducks, looks for coats, finds shelter. I stand in the storm.

Ed leads Libby away, and they are huddled together, talking, Ed trying to calm her. I can see their decision: They didn't want to tell the truth, the whole truth, which is that there are illegals missing on their property, that Ed has been involved. Now they will. Too much is at stake. I see them nod, hold each other's hands, walk toward the officers.

"No, wait," I holler. I jog up to them and pant. "Don't tell them. Not yet. Just wait a half an hour." I jump in Kay's truck and peel out before anyone can stop me, and the rearview mirror tells me that the officers aren't following. The roads are dark and empty and cold.

Please, Amber, where are you?

THINK, TESS, THINK

Go toward the danger.

If you can't stay clear, entirely clear, go *toward* the danger. Meet it headon.

That's the advice I gave her, and given the choice, that's the advice she'll follow. It's the advice I will follow too.

Chapter Seventeen

The reservoir is the only holdingplace for water around here, and therefore all life gravitates toward it, pulled to the magnetic draw of water. Deer. Birds. Groves of trees. Families. Men seeking something to do for the day. In the expanse of shoreline and tamarisk and sandstone outcroppings, it's not easy to find anyone, but I know Slade's rule of thumb: Always head west. If anything ever happens, he always advised, go one bar or one street or one town or one valley west. The direction west offered up the most hope, so we set it to the center of our compass.

The east side is the state campground anyway, and it's where the water is released in the stilling pond and then the Arkansas River starts up again. Here on the west side, where the river runs thick and salty in the reservoir, the landscape is wild. I'm driving so fast on the two-rut dirt road that the truck is bucking all over the place, bouncing my skull into my neckbones, bouncing the headlights around in the dark. It's the stout buffalo grass, thick in bunches, that sends the truck jolting so wildly. I can only see what the headlights reveal, but I know I'm passing the campgrounds, pullouts, a sandy beach, a rocky area, another beach. The howling wind is picking up, and a short burst of snow-hail spits from the sky. I see one vehicle, but when I pull up to look over, I see it's a foggedup teenager car. I blink back the sting in my eyes, because, oh, god, it suddenly feels like the whole world is a huge expanse of space that seems to go on and on, and in which you'd find no one if she weren't waving her arms or whistling.

Finally, a glint. My headlights catch the chrome of something, and I pull slowly forward. Hallelujah. It's Slade's black truck with the topper. He's driven over a gully of rocks, where the sandstone has cleaved off, into a low-lying area—to hide and be hidden. I doubt Kay's truck will make it. Not enough clearance, not enough power to get me out of it. I turn off the ignition and jump out of the truck and start running and then pull myself up short. Always assess a situation before approach.

I slow, walk quietly, carefully. There are the sandstone cliffs up ahead. I showed them to Slade, once, this being the secret spot only locals know about, where there are old Indian writings and marks left by the conquistadors, too. Coronado, in fact. I stop to get a good read on the situation, and at the same time the moon reveals itself, and so I can see the outline of the bursts of sandstone cliffs, rocky and jangly. Up ahead, the tamarack and cottonwoods and weeds and salt grass are thick, and the air smells of it. Musky from the dry rot of fall, dense with the Arkansas River that enters the reservoir here, the water that started so clean up in the mountains and has ended up so thick by the time it reaches here. I trip over tumbleweeds and have to weave through the kochia, and my feet sink into the silty clay soil. It's sticky and tacky, as if it's trying to bur me to it. To my left, toward the reservoir, the soil spreads out flat and is burned with the pattern of thick cracks that crisscross and form little maps.

A pheasant explodes out of the grass, a flash in the moonlight, startling me back into movement. I approach Slade's truck. The campfire is nearly out; the truck, both the cab and the back, are empty. I whistle, the sound of a canyon wren: *cui-da-do.* Whistle. No answer. Whistle. But not even a whistle carries through this much noise.

There are no footprints left and just the smallest light and crackle from the fire. There's a single shoe, old and dusty, but that could be from anyone at any time. I look around, listen. Nothing. I approach and unhinge the latch and climb quietly into the back of the truck. There's Slade's empty sleeping bag, the wool blankets, his peagreen jacket. There's a paper bag fallen over with some oranges rolling out. I dig around for his headlamp and click it on, and a cloud of breath hangs in the air at the edge of the light. I gotta think. Gotta make a list:

Slade: hired by Lobo for transport.

Me: the transport.

Mota and *coca* burned in the fire.

But only one dead body.

Oh, god, I see it now.

Lobo heard there was only one Mexican national found. He assumes the others survived. Therefore, they have the *coca y mota.* He thinks I staged it. He thinks I started a fire, ran with the drugs. This is Lobo's logic. Lobo thinks: No one in their fucking right mind would leave so much money in the mountains.

The yelp of a woman pierces the air. I lie back fast, click off the headlamp, pull the sleeping bag over me. Did they see my truck? No, they're coming from the opposite direction, from the direction of the place where the river enters the reservoir. I pull myself up so I can look out the window. It's hard to see, although there are headlamps illuminating a group. Alejandra. A limping woman: Lupe. The group of men. Being pushed by a man I can't see.

My heart is skipping all over the place, pounding to get out, pounding for me to get out of this truck. The heat in my core is rising, rising, burning me apart. My hands start to shake on their own.

Then I hear it. The whistle back. *Cui-da-do*. Slade's seen my truck. Or he somehow hopes I'm here.

"Hey, shutthefuck up." A low voice, Mexican. "*Siéntense todos, y cierren el pico. Sit down and shut up.*"

More talking. It's hard for me to tell who's who. But then I hear someone curse, and it is the gravel-voice of Lobo himself. Lobo is here, and he has Amber. He has Alejandra. He has Lupe. He has Slade.

"Hey, you. Fuckhead." It's Lobo's voice, coming from the side of the truck. "I want you to call Tess."

Amber: Crying. "She doesn't have a phone—"

Slade: "I told you, man, she doesn't have a phone. And we didn't know—"

Lobo: "How were you planning on getting a hold of her? Huh?" A punch, a gasp for air. The struggle for an intake of breath.

Slade: "Jesus, man. I told you. She was going to come up here. I was in no hurry. We left it loose, man. She was gonna hang with her family. And then, when she was ready, she was just gonna come up—" and more punching, more gasping for air.

Two guns will be up front, locked in a box that Slade keeps behind his seat. But mine is here. Oh, god, thank you. The Colt .38. *Salvador.* It will still be unloaded, but the cartridge box will be wrapped in the same soft cloth. My hand searches by itself in the dark. I close my eyes to concentrate. There's a scuffle outside, and I peer carefully out the window. People are being pushed down to sit near the fire. I can only see old Lupe, her hands tied behind her, hunched forward, and all I can hear is the wind, howling, dirt and pebbles hitting the side of the truck.

I make myself go slow. Count to ten. Think of Amber's face. Slowly, I move my hand past flares and water-purifying tablets and finally over the smooth soft cloth. Unwrap it. Grab onto the gun.

I wrap my fingers around the small gun, think of the times that

Slade has made me practice, how he always said, *This gun is perfect for you, baby.* But it's dark, and my hands are shaking. Tears start to fau-cetdrip out of my eyes. Such a bad time for it. A bad time to feel. I need to turn the emotions off.

I hear Alejandra yelp. My body is going to buzz apart. Crack apart. Explode. Alejandra yells, *Get off me*, and I am calm. Calm with a rage inside me.

You were ready to die before.
Now do it with a purpose.
Hang tight, dearheart.
Do it, Tess.
Load it.
Slide and turn the cylinder.
Slide and turn the cylinder. Six times. Six shots.

Single action. Cock it with your thumb.

It will jump.
Left hand holds right hand,
right index finger near the trigger,
shoot for chest area.
(Slade said: It will be harder than you think,
not Hollywood.
Much harder if they're moving.
Assume you won't hit him unless you're close.
Shoot to kill.)

(Get directly in front, as close as you can.)

(Lower aim a bit, you're always high.)

(Once it's cocked, it's live.)

(If worse comes to worse, Slade used to say, you need to
know this, Tess: You need to shoot to kill.
It's the life you've chosen, and you need to know it. And for
god's sake, don't forget about the safety.)

My fingers slide the bullets in.

Chapter Eighteen

I close my eyes to center myself with one last full breath, and the memory of Libby giving me this gun sweeps into my mind. Amber had been born, my bags were packed, my resolve was steady, and we were standing outside the old home. She handed me her Colt .38, which she'd gotten from her best friend Shawny, who had used it on herself, and she said, "Kidsister, learn to use it, because you're heading out into a life that is bigger and scarier than you think."

Lupe screams. *No. NO.*

And I'd said to her, "You're heading into a life bigger and scarier than *you* think," and as I said this, my eyes had drifted over to Amber, tucked into a car seat, sleeping, and I reached out and took the small gun in my hand.

Amber sobs, *Please let me go home, please.*

And Libby had grabbed my wrist and said, "Promise me on all that we ever shared together that you will not use this gun on yourself. Because that would kill me."

And I'd promised.

And she'd said, "Tess, listen to me. If you ever get close . . . come home and visit me first. Promise me. I wish I had told Shawny that. If ever she got close . . . to talk to me first. We could have figured something out. So don't you ever do that to me. You come to me first. Okay?"

And I'd promised again and thought, This bigsister has no idea what she's talking about because I'm in for a life of fun and adventure. I'm in a life for all that is beautiful and bold and exciting. She's the one who is dying.

And it is only striking me now: That she has known why I came back, and I have known why I came back, but neither of our minds believed it until right now.

*

I exhale the breath. Out the window I see dark figures gathered around a small fire, heads ducked against the wind, and I hear bits of discussion about moving people to a van that must be nearby. My eyes search the group. I need to identify where Amber is, where Alejandra is. I can't make them out, and my eyes move from one shape to another, and finally I see Alejandra, on the outskirts, being tugged off to the side, toward a cluster of trees.

I cannot see Lobo, but I know he's to the left. The man to my right is still pulling Alejandra. Slowly, slowly, slowly. I start to turn the latch; Lupe screams, *Mi hija*; and I hear a man saying, *Fuck you, bitch.* And right before the final click, I stop my hand. The universe is telling me something. Listen. Oh, I hear it: I know what the man is thinking at this very moment in time. He'd rather take her in the truck. Warm and comfortable. I watch him make the decision. Turn in the other direction. Toward me. Here, in the truckbed, with the topper, it will be better. He doesn't want to be cold and windblown either.

I back away from the door with a certain silent speed. I get my gun up, cock it with my thumb, my left hand supporting my right. The man is struggling with the latch, struggling with the effort of holding a strong young person who is thrashing around, and she tumbles away from him. As he turns to catch her and heave her up, my body tries to shy away, to turn to the side, and I hear the universe loud and clear: *Move toward the danger.* I force my body back in front of him, and as he opens the window, I look him in the face and shoot. There is an explosion both of bullet and of bone, and I am sprayed with wet.

*

I jump from the truck in one move and turn toward Lobo, who is turning to me. I point the gun at him, lower it, and there is an explosion and he is still standing there staring at me and I know I have missed and now he is reaching for his gun and I walk toward him, straight up to him. I reposition the gun, reposition my hands on the gun, bring a gust of air into my body and hold it. I shoot, and he flies back.

I hear Slade, *One more there's one more!* and then Slade is standing up, his hands tied behind him, and he is yelling, *Run, girls! Sálvense! Corran!* and he is barreling toward another man who I just now see, a man who had been sitting in the shadows, with his gun trained on me, and by the time I see him I know he has already fired and

Slowly, slowly.

Time moves this way, and you know that entire universes
are held in the breath of a second.

The man pushes Slade off of him and is getting his balance. I am on my knees, sinking, I raise the gun to shoot. Left hand holding right hand, finger to trigger. Our eyes touch. Across space. He turns and starts running. Into the night. A scream. The wind, a woman, a human soul.

I stay on my knees. Should I shoot him in the back? No. I lower the gun. He is a no-one, like me, someone who couldn't feel, who didn't mean to start trouble, a fire or a death; he just hadn't thought about it because he couldn't feel about it, and he is gone.

*

Noises pierce me all at once:

    The cracking of burning logs at the fire.

    Slade writhing on the ground, moaning.

    Lobo on the ground, gurgling.

    A sound of weeping.

    An owl somewhere in the far distance.

    The buzz of silence from the night sky. The roar of stars.

    I crouch down. There is no cell phone anywhere in the dead guy's jacket. I move toward Lobo, alive and mumbling, and I think of the woman's dead body that I did see,

        the bones and red barrette,

        Kay's dead body, just lying there silent in a room.

    I hold it all in my head, in my universe, and I move toward Lobo and kick away the gun near his arm, and though he is alive, I feel his jacket, over his chest, on his sides, and yes, there, next to him, on the ground, is the shape of what I'm looking for. I flick it on and my hands are shaking and the whole world's thoughts crash on me at once:

    Stop Slade's bleeding,

    find Amber,

    check on the others,

    there's one more man out there,

    keep the gun at your side,

    stay low.

    But I need to focus on the first thing on the list, this one call, reaching out like a prayer.

"It's badbadbad," I say into the phone, teeth chattering, bone crashing bone. "Southwest side of the dam."

Dispatcher: "Where is the girl?"

Me: "I'm looking." I walk on my knees to Slade and am taking off my shirt and holding it to Slade's side, but my eyes are furious in their search to my right. "Amber. Where is she, where is she?"

Slade: "Oh fuck it hurts like fuck."

Me into the phone: "The reservoir, west side, rock outcrop, ambulance, Amber."

I am shaking so hard, and before I crunch down to die in it, I look around again. Where is everyone? Alejandra and Lupe and the others are gone. There is one extra shape and a noise I have not yet checked on.

Amber?

I crawl over to it, my kneebones against rock, and then say it again, but the shape doesn't answer. I reach out and tap it with my hand. It is Amber, staring up at me. Not crying, not anything, just dead with fright.

"Oh, Amber." I lower my gun, bend, curl up beside her. "They're gone, they're gone." I hold her to me, and I think of me reaching in for that unborn baby's skull, how the little bones fell like insect wings.

"I want my mom. I want my dad." Her voice is faint, and her body is jerking and hiccupping and coughing and vibrating now, suddenly coming alive.

"She's coming, Amber. They're all coming. They're on their way—"

I bend my body around her in the echoing darkness, and she is gasping for breath now between great sobs and screams.

There is a hand. I look up: Alejandra's face right above mine. "We are fine," she whispers. "We are leaving. The men got our wrists free. I hear the sirens, and help is coming. We cannot get caught and sent back now. We've tried too hard. Goodbye, *mi mamá*."

I nod and put my head back down on earth and curl tighter into Amber. The endless murmuring of all my selves tells me that we are two creatures, not one. I could staunch Slade's blood better, yell into the night and call for Alejandra to come back. But no. I will hold Amber, form a curve around her on these stones that fuse into a single planet, into the nest of my body. I will hold her as the cold pulses of the stars thrum in the sky. I will hold her tight on this red earth.

PART V

Earth

Chapter Nineteen

The highway has me thinking. A new theory sweeps into my mind as we pull off the pavement and park the cars and trucks at the farmhouse, and the simplicity of it makes me laugh out loud, randomly, startling everyone as we gather and hunch together in the chill of a clouded day. My theory is simply this: Here, at my mother's funeral, at the moment we are honoring her departure from her body, I understand something about bodies in general. That a good-feeling body clarifies the brain in wondrous and elemental ways. Who knew? That one was so dependent upon the other? *Oh!* I keep thinking over and over. *Of course! This is what it feels like to be in a body that doesn't hurt, this is what it feels like to have the brain clear, of course!* Medicines and rest have taken away the blur and roars and stings that lived in my tooth, in my crotch, in my stomach, in my bones. The nerves have calmed. Weight has lifted. Such a strange, radiant surprise. There is more sweeping that needs to be done in my body, yes, more to be released or attended to, but it keeps surprising me. I forgot what it feels like to be in a body that has been cleaned. For too long, I have lived in a cluttered, messy home, full of too many pangs and aches.

When I laugh, everyone turns to me: Libby, Amber, Ed, Charlene from the grocery, a few of the ranchers from nearby, and Miguel, who had overlooked the fact that Libby had whispered to him about the others involved, people who had disappeared into the night. Who knows what the law will discover, but our story is a solid one, the truth except for the existence of Alejandra and Lupe and the others. The wind has taken away their footprints, the stories have taken away their presence. Funny, how so much can remain invisible.

As Libby and I walk away from the others for this last final gesture, out into the pasture with the urn, I wonder if Planet Earth ever feels the same as my body does. Lousy, but then, at some moments, a little clearer and calmer. For example, how the winds brought in a snowstorm that hit in the mountains that very night, and the wildfire is now contained. Not out, but contained, and with new snowstorms on the way. I wonder if the earth feels how, for at least a while, some elemental order has been established.

Perhaps the people of the mountains are feeling better, too. It's true there have been great sorrows: The remains of the homeowner have been found. She had received a reverse 911 call but had refused to leave. The body of Oscar will be returned to his family in Mexico. A small group of people near Alamosa have made new signs, *No más cruces en la frontera*, to acknowledge and mark the problem, to say, *We notice*. Ranchers are in the process of finding their animals, people are starting the process of rebuilding their homes. The grief is alive and burbling, I am sure, but at least things have calmed enough to allow *for* the grief.

Libby and I walk over sage and grass and cottonwood leaves that are dusted in a light small-flaked snow. As soon as we're out of earshot, I say, "Libby, I'm sorry. Thank you for not abandoning me completely."

Libby releases a strange sad laugh and keeps her eyes on the blue urn she is carrying. "Well, Tess. It's gonna take a while. You nearly got my daughter killed. Let's just get through this funeral. Let's just get through today. We can at least do this together."

I watch shoes, mine red, hers white, step over sage, cactus, yucca. "Well, there's one thing I know how to say: I love you. And I ask to be forgiven. I know such a thing won't come now, or easily, or maybe ever, but I still need to ask. I never thought Lobo would come—"

"I know." Her voice has the edge of bitterness in its quiet murmur.

"I'm going to try harder. If it's any consolation."

Ringo has darted from the group behind us and is now circling our legs, tail wagging. He trots ahead, his pads leaving sweet marks on the frost. He looks back, grows impatient, and comes back for us.

Libby holds Kay's urn up a little, as if raising it for a toast. "Remember that time when we jumped off a tractor and landed on some old metal? And we both had deep cuts on our legs? Blood all over the place. We tried to hide it, to rub it off with our socks, but it kept going. We needed stitches. So finally we ran back to the house, to Kay, and we were so scared. She was standing on the porch, smoking a cigarette, and even though I was the older one, you approached her first and said, 'You can get mad at us later, but help us now.'"

I laugh quietly. "That's kind of how I felt, coming back here," I say after a pause. "Get mad later, but help me first. Must be the call of those in true distress." Then I nudge her gently with my elbow and nod to the red thrust of a rock outcrop. "Is here where she wanted?" Here, near a small creek, a cluster of cottonwoods gather, and the last yellowed leaves flutter like a pirate flag on an old ship.

"Yes, here." Libby looks at me; we both nod. "Ready?"

"Hang on a second." I stand and do a slowmotion spin to look at the pasturelands and cluster of outbuildings and the earth around me and then settle on looking west. There is the blur of mountains, now dusted in white and hard to distinguish from the white sky. Up above them, I know, are stars, even though they are obscured by light, and above them, the universe, spiraling in a galaxy full of spirals and sequences, of lost and found blooms of red stars and possibility.

I tap my chestbone. Inside is something just as vast. Inside is a galaxy, and it accounts for the emotions that make a mother scream, that make a child cry, the yearning for connection, the rise of lust, the ache of lonely, and, yes, the constant-burn energy of whatever it is that heals, whatever it is that makes us laugh in joy.

I nod to Libby, and we both put our hands on the urn. When we fling the ashes up and away from us, a gust of wind picks up the ash and takes it right back into our faces. I gasp, duck. The grit slaps me across my cheek, flies into my eyes. I stand there stunned: Kay's bone dust in my mouth, in my eyes, in my nostrils, and I circle around, pawing at my face and tongue. Ringo runs over to me, bounding around my legs in my own confusion, jumps up hard enough to claw me through my jeans, and then I am doubled over with the pain of that. I rub my face, my scalp, my hair. But then I look over at Libby, and she is bent over, her body heaving, so I stumble over to her and pull her to me to help. That's when I see she is laughing.

"That's so Kay," she's gasping. "That's so Kay."

I blink, and we stand there, holding each other and rocking back and forth, me muttering *Fuck*, and her laughing, and the both of us spitting dust from our mouths. Our faces are streaked with whitegray, her eyelashes especially. We back up, eventually, and brush off each other's shoulders and hair. She tilts her head at me, holds her palm to my face. "Tess, this will be hard to work through. It's not going to be easy. Amber can't turn out like you. You understand?"

"Yes."

"You need to help her. Don't go running off on me now. You need to stay and be a warm presence, a steady influence, a good person. If you leave, I want you to know, you'd no longer have a home here. You'd no longer be welcome."

I hold her hand that is holding my cheek, look her in the eye. "Yes. I feel that too. I got my feet pointed in the damn right direction, and that involves staying put."

Then we hold hands and look back at the others. We pause for a moment to watch the rest of Kay blow off of us and out of the urn and off the sage and grass at our feet, mixing into the white dust of the frost. The larger bits settle in among the dirt and rocks, a beetle scuttles away, a cottonwood leaf drips from a tree. The temperature is just rising enough that the frost is starting to bead into moisture. The ancient impatience of water, right next to the ancient impatience of the human heart.

Chapter Twenty

Alejandra pulls up the sleeves of her yellow fleece jacket so that she can show me her wrists. They're rubbed raw, bruised, in places welted and in other places scratched like my cheek. I wince, run my finger alongside the wounds. "And inside? Your heart?"

We're sitting under the same cottonwood outside the old Earthship, settling ourselves down among the roots. The clouds have rambled on, and the sun's afternoon gold is rolling out across the land. I look at the curve of our knees, our shoes on the yellow leaves. Her moccasins and my red tennis shoes make me think of all the traveling we have done.

She leans her head against my shoulder, holds my hand. "That will take some time. I miss Oscar."

"Yes." My voice feels as worn and soft as a wasp nest. "I'm so sorry."

"We were going to make a home together. I'm tired of looking for a home."

"Well, there's here. There's me."

She laces her fingers with mine. "Yes, perhaps. For a while." Then she adds, "I can't stop thinking of the fire. I believe I'll feel guilty for the rest of my life."

I bring her fingers to my mouth and kiss her knuckles. "We need to fix this. This running back and forth, these countries that make a person do such a thing. There needs to be a better way."

We both nod, quiet in the thoughts of our small selves within this large canvas. Finally, I sigh. "Will you be okay? Amber and I are going into Lamar for therapy. Together and separately. It will be important. I worry that she'll become hard, like me, and so will you."

She looks up at me, smiles. "We have Libby's trained hand, Ed's wisdom, your streetsmarts. We were going to drive off, you know. Go to Minnesota or Montana or who knows! Just go and go. But then we realized, I think, that no one would know. We were *still* a secret. Even after all this. And driving that van might be more dangerous than sticking close. I think you taught us that, once. How sometimes the safest place to be is right near the danger."

I gaze off across the land. Amber's 4-H cows have wandered from the pasture near the house and into this one, and one is close up, knees folded under hulking body. She stops chewing her cud long enough to reach her tongue up and lick out her nose. "They're investigating, of course. But we are all on one page on how the story goes, and it does not involve you. The truth except for the part that involves all of you." I hold her hand. "You could stay, you know. Help with Kay's house. Because, you know, Kay wanted to use the house and acreage for something good. Perhaps it can become another secret safe house, for example. For the lost and found among us. It's perfect. So remote."

We talk of the future, then. They plan on staying, she tells me, for at least a while. But given that every human wants to do something of value, and that simply sitting and waiting and hiding will never be enough, their departure might come soon. "Perhaps *mi madre* will stay and raise chickens and help with the bees. But the rest of us. I think we want to move on into our lives. Kay's will be a good place for all the broken things that need to heal. But we'll see. Something else is calling to me. I need to listen. I just don't know what I'm hearing quite yet."

My lips open, and I want to say something to her. Something I have always wanted to say but could not find or invent the right words. Something about the vacuum of a realization that fell into my heart the moment I saw her. Something about how if we listen harder, stare harder, focus harder, use our imaginations harder, the people at the other end of our sight, well, they morph from blurs on the horizon, something barely discernible at a distance, and become very clear, very detailed. How all of us, each of us, are waving our arms, trying to attract attention. Our hands are cupped around our mouths in a whistle. Our faces are red from the effort. We are wanting to tell our story, be specific, to share a language. We only need someone to see and to listen and to feel, and our shapes take form.

I pull her toward me and finger her black hair, twisting it and then letting it spiral out, and then, as she used to say as a child, repeati-fying it. She curls against me and naps, and the earth beneath us seems solid and firm and unchanging. The land is enough to hold us. All the land, it seems, is here to hold us.

Chapter Twenty-One

Slade's hospital room smells like lemon and sage, and he's in the wheelchair with a dufflebag on his lap and a nurse holding up medicine bottles, one by one, and explaining. Underneath his flannel shirt are broken ribs and a gunshot wound that turned out to be a bad scrape and tissue damage. The wound looks like a crack in the dirt, the lines on a map, and as I gingerly touched the area yesterday, I thought, *Yet another example of how so much depends on such a small fraction of a moment.*

I lean against the wall and watch him while he signs papers and gets instructions. He runs his hand along the edge of his beard every time he looks overwhelmed or confused. He wants out, the big baby. Terrified he'll get a staph infection there, having heard about Kay's trauma. Terrified because he's never been good at being in closed spaces and small rooms.

He couldn't believe it, he told me when I first visited him, he just couldn't believe it when Lobo showed up with Lupe and Alejandra and the others. He was fishing at the dam, having a beer and sitting in a lawn chair, when all of a sudden he got clocked over the head with a rock. While he was falling, in that fraction of a moment, he looked up and saw Lobo, and Lobo said, "I put a sticker GPS locator on your truck, you fool. I'd never trust you. You're too good to be trusted," and Slade thought, *I need to prepare to die.*

Lobo believed we had staged the whole thing. That Slade or I had started the fire and taken off with the product. Lobo had used the GPS locator sticker on Slade's pickup to get our general vicinity. While driving up and down the county roads, he came across a unique glassed home, and they stopped to rob it, figuring money or art or something valuable would be inside. Indeed, there was. Because the girl who came out of the door had tried to move toward the danger by saying, "If you're looking for Tess, then you should know that she's quit this business," which was just enough information for him to chase her into the house and around the table, grab her, and put her in the truck. In the end, she'd learned enough from climbing cottonwood trees in the pasture and overhearing tidbits of conversation to know that someone was hiding out at the old Earthship house, and so, desperate for her life, she directed Lobo there. And Alejandra, once caught, also desperate for her life, directed them to the old house, where they found Slade's note to me. Now they had everyone they needed to hold ransom. It was like a treasure hunt. Clues being left here and there, all of us pirates, seeking our own version of treasure.

*

As soon as the nurse gives me the nod, I walk toward Slade in his scruffle-bearded handsome wonder. Sure enough, his eyes light when he sees me. I bend down and hug him. "Ready to get outta here?"

He grunts, pats my back, meaning, he's too close to tears to be able to speak.

"The germs are coming to get you," I tease, fluttering my hands at him. But he is in pain, and so I touch his cheeks and kiss him tenderly. Something I've never seen startles me, which is a slow drip of tears running down the crease of his nose.

I use my thumbs to smear in the smooth silk of water into the landscape of his face.

Dr. Lemon steps in the room. "You both got your meds? You are both coming back tomorrow?" He means the antianxiety pills he prescribed, he means the trauma counseling we are signed up for in the coming days. His voice is chirpy, and there is a light in his eyes despite the words. "Like I said yesterday, people don't shoot one another and go on with their lives as if nothing happened. You have work to do, my friends." With that, he nods at the little computer he carries with him on his rounds and darts off.

I wheel Slade around the corridors until we reach the entrance, the nurse following behind. Once we're through the doors, he has to stand so she can take the chair back. I hold him at the elbow and guide him toward the parking lot. "Baxter was always offering me good wisdoms, some of which are only starting to make sense now," I tell him as we shuffle along. "Once he told me, 'The young in the world are crazy for light and the old are afraid it's leaving them.' I like that. I wonder about the middle, though. The light we're grasping for is a bit like noon, isn't it? Hard light, but we sure appreciate it."

He shuffles along, clearly in pain and on drugs, until we make it to Kay's truck. "I think it's hard noon now, because my ribs hurt." He chuckles, winces. "So, to Kay's house?"

"Till you're off the pain meds." I stand in front of him so that he can't yet maneuver himself into the truck. I reach up to stroke his chin, the scruffle that borders shaven territory from unshaven. "Before we go to Kay's, I have to tell you something. I have to do it now, or I won't have the courage to do it at all."

"I know what you're going to say, Tess—"

"Well, let me say it anyway. I need to learn to use the words. Slade, I used to believe that love just came to you. That it wasn't love if you had to work for it. But that's not true, is it? I'm just now understanding that. For some reason, I thought that if you worked for it, it wasn't real."

He cups my chin, tilts it, holds my gaze. Hoists an eyebrow. "I'm not sure that rules me out, though."

A yellowjacket flies by us, and I bat it away from him. Above us, the geese are migrating south, their calls a language something half-whispered and half-sung. "Maybe it doesn't make sense. But many things don't make sense, I'm realizing. I have to learn how to feel. I have to do that alone. When I drove out of here ten years ago, I think I was trying to make life fit my idea of what it was supposed to be. To bend it to the idea that I had in mind. But then I made life give and take more than it could."

He looks over my shoulder at the horizon. "You can see the mountains today. Did you notice that? They're snowcapped. And don't you think that those emotions are the sort of thing that grows? We're war buddies, after all. People don't go through this kind of stuff without . . . Don't you think it would be nice to have someone who has seen the same shit? Who can care for you despite? It's the dark corners, maybe, that we can most love?"

I move my hands to rub the edge of his beard, his temples, push my hands into his hair. "Yes. Some love grows. I didn't love Amber when I had her. I think I love her now, but I'm also too messed up to know. I need to settle. Settle in order to feel. That's true for what I feel for you, too. I don't suppose you want to come back in a year? Next fall, when the leaves are turning?"

He runs his hands across my cheeks and smiles sadly. Holds me away from him so he can look me in the eyes and then holds me to him, rocks back and forth. "You sure do have some eyes there," I hear him murmur. Then, "What do I have? About three days? Three days to convince you?"

I laugh, the carbonated prayer type, and step back and kick at the black asphalt with the red tennis shoes. The cracks in the parking lot look like a map, like trails taking him somewhere new, and my crumble of asphalt goes tumbling along them. "No, you're leaving. What will you do?"

He sighs but smiles. "Move to Mexico. I'm not going to tell you where, though. I don't want you to know, because then you'd feel obligated to keep a secret." He reaches out and moves a bit of hair and tucks it behind my ear.

I kick another crumble of asphalt. "Darlingsweet, I suppose we all need to start new lives somewhere."

He breathes out, resigned. "I'd like to write you, though. I'll use Libby's address, because no matter where _you_ go now, you'll stay in touch."

I nod. "Yes, that's true."

"And you? I'm guessing that . . . killing . . . isn't as easy to absorb as one would think. Even if he was a dangerous shithead . . . and he was, Tess, both the guy who was taking Alejandra to the truck and Lobo. I'm glad they're dead. Those guys were messed up."

The sky is squawking with a clearblue that pulses light, just like on the day I arrived. "Yes. I want to let the winter come down around me and just . . . hold me. I need to make some peace. Connect myself. Put the puzzle pieces back together. Merge. Solidify. I need to find the ways to leave my worst self and find my better one. A unified better one."

I press my head into his chest, and we stand like this in the parking lot for a long time. How can I explain it? I need to find a path that leads to some sort of purpose, to mitigate the fact that the human race evolved or got plunked down to wonder and suffer and be afraid of death, and afraid of pain—afraid because we don't know how to live this life, and not certain if we're being judged, and if we are, by what elements? It's in the wondering itself that I'll find redemption in the red earth and the howl of coyotes and the blue sky.

Chapter Twenty-Two

Before I walk into the multisplendored house, with its bottles and cans and glass sparkling in the evening light, I stop to look west, toward the sunset with the waves of blue topped with streaks of orange and red. The heavens are humming, I think to myself, and later the sky will harden, but right now they are offering a soft, lilting music. I breathe in, a last call for bravery.

As soon as I step into the door, I see Amber sitting at the kitchen table, piling items on the bright tablecloth. I pause, startled. She's holding an old newspaper, and it strikes me as familiar, and I have to cock my head and listen to my memories in order to place it.

Then I remember. When I first left, I *did* send Libby one package. I had gone into some touristy gift shop in Durango and bought a fake *Durango Times* where you could write your own headlines. The headline reads, TESS ESCAPES! and in smaller print below, KID SISTER CROSSES BORDER TO NEW LIFE! And then there is just random type, that makes no sense, and then there are smaller headlines, put there by the store: TWO-HEADED COW LEFT BY ALIENS, and BEAR ATTACKS CRIMINAL, HELPS POLICE.

Amber looks up at me, then down at the large plastic box she's holding. "Remember this?"

"Yes."

"This is some stuff my mom saved." She reaches her arm toward me, handing me a piece of notebook paper. I walk in the house and take it carefully from her. It's Libby's handwriting, one of her many lists, written while Amber bloomed in my stomach:

REASONS I WANT TO ADOPT TESS'S BABY AFTER
IT IS BORN:

—BECAUSE TESS DIDN'T REALLY WANT TO HAVE
  AN ABORTION EVEN THOUGH SHE SAID IT WAS
  OKAY. PLUS WE DON'T HAVE THE MONEY. PLUS
  WE WERE SCARED.

—BECAUSE IT WOULD MAKE TESS PROUD.

—BECAUSE IT WOULD MAKE ME SPECIAL.

—BECAUSE I WANT SOMETHING TO HAPPEN IN
  MY LIFE.

—BECAUSE I WANT SOMEONE TO LOVE ME. JUST ME.

—BECAUSE I DON'T KNOW WHAT MY LIFE IS ABOUT.
  ESPECIALLY IF IT'S NOT ABOUT TESS.

—I WANT TO BE BRAVE ENOUGH TO REACH
  FOR SOMETHING TERRIFIC WHILE I HAVE
  THE CHANCE.

—BECAUSE I KNOW TESS IS GOING TO LEAVE. AND
MAYBE IF I KEEP HER BABY, SHE'LL STICK AROUND.
OR COME BACK.

I look up out the window, toward the mountains. "She was brave.
And you are terrific."

Amber bites her lower lip, and her nose scrunches in response.
"And you came back."

"Yes. And I'm staying through the winter, even if you and Ed and
Libby are all mad at me, which you should be."

"For bringing all this holyhell here?"

I laugh. For her made-up words, for her face, teasing. "Yes."

"For traumatizedsoul? For permanent-scar?"

I take her hand. "We shouldn't be laughing. It's serious. Like I
said before, you have to be careful what you witness. But then, look
what I did to you! That's one reason I want to stay, Amber. To see if I
can be of any help. I'm so sorry."

Her face grows quiet. "Yes," she says. "I haven't been feeling so
good. You're right about what you see. But like you once told my mom,
you have to be careful not to live a small life. We should all be living
more dangerous lives, you said. If you get *too* careful, you get small."
Then, "She'll forgive you, maybe. If you stick around and are useful
and giving for once. I'll forgive you too. I think."

"Really? I'm not sure you know what that means—"

She is interrupted by a sound from behind us, though, and I turn,
expecting to see Ed or Libby. It is Alejandra, listening quietly from the
door. "May I . . . ?"

I open my mouth to say something, but Amber is faster. "Hi,
Alejandra." She moves toward Alejandra, and they hug each other tight.

Oh! Oh, yes, *of course.* Of course. I stare at them, startled by the
sudden realization that they have gone through this together. Amber

now knows about the group, that they are at the old Earthship. These two girls are now bound together for life. This girl whom I gave motherlove will now offer motherlove to my other child. I saved Alejandra from the trauma of the daytime desert, she now will save Amber from the trauma of a certain night. Because of this, they will never be able to turn away from the real sorrows of the world. They will use it to their advantage and to become more human.

Now they are turning away from me, not registering my startle, and they are mumbling something about making a cake. A TessHoneyCake, Amber is saying with a giggle. And now Alejandra is humming the song her mother was singing. Then Libby walks in, carrying a heavy wooden bucket. "Hello, dearhearts," she says to Amber and Alejandra. "It's time to get busy, everyone. We're finally going to spin the honey out. Ed's bringing the frames in."

She puts down the bucket with a thud and turns in my direction, offers a small smile. In return, I offer a small wave of the hand. Such a small movement with such potential, and now each of us standing in a new and settled silence. She looks to me like a thirty-year-old small-town woman should look, her thick hair pulled back in a raggedy ponytail, an oversized white T-shirt and cheapbrand jeans. She looks like someone who has sailed with open eyes through the suffering this world offers.

I look past her to the kitchen to see the empty jars, waiting to be filled. Soon we will be carving off the caps of wax with a hot knife, putting the thin frames into the spinner, and the honey will leak out, fall, drip down into a big bucket like faucet-branches. Little molecules, like our separate selves, pouring together and uniting and glowing. Like the dance of yellow cottonwoodleaves. Like waves of golden wheat running. As water is the sea.

Out the window, I see the sky is offering a small dancing snow, evidence of the change that is to come. The flakes spin in several directions, currents pushing the snow sideways. That same sky that offered us red lightning is now offering to coat the world in a fine bonewhite dust.

Oh, Tess.

You can find the flesh

that covers the bones.

Brave people are kind people.

Courage is opening your arms, nodding hello to the difficult universe,

to wind, water, fire, air, earth.

I look at Amber, Alejandra, Libby, gathered in the kitchen. Ed and Slade are coming through the door, chuckling over something. What would be the point in a life without them? I take a step toward it all.

Acknowledgments

Air: With deep gratitude to those who offered wisdoms on the words: Dan Smetanka, Jody Kahn, Laura Resau, Karye Cattrell, Mary Dean, Rick Bass.

Water: For those who sustained with friendship and support: Kurt Gutjahr, James Pritchett, Barbara Clark, Sandra Deraney Reilly, Kent Haruf, Jake Pritchett, Eliana Pritchett.

Earth: To UCross and Earthskin Muriwai for offering a place and sanctuary.

Fire: With deep thanks for those who offered stories and wisdoms on the details: Carol Guerrero-Murphy, Sophia Guerrero-Murphy, David Guerrero, Aaron Abeyta, Debbie Hayhow, Julia Davis, Morgan Smith, Angie Huntley Austin, Lynette Vialet, Luiz Neves, and the people who need to remain anonymous but who are never invisible.

Wind: To all those who have crossed borders of one kind or another.

Printed in the United States
by Baker & Taylor Publisher Services